Welcome to our 2025 collection, *Work: An Anthology of Suffolk Stories*. This is the first volume in our new series, following the highly successful four-book series of anthologies from the Creative and Critical Writing postgraduate students at the University of Suffolk.

Our anthologies focus on the importance of place in storytelling, with each original short story set in and inspired by a specific location in East Anglia. Our first anthology, *Suffolk Folk* (2021) draws on local myth and folktales as inspiration. The second anthology, *Suffolk Arboretum* (2022) explores the ancient trees and woodlands of our region. *Suffolk Reflections* (2023) traces the inland and coastal waters of East Anglia, while *Suffolk Haunts* (2024), the last book of the series, shares glorious tales of ghosts and local superstition.

Five years on, this anthology marks a continuation of talented storytelling by our MA students, and a new beginning. *Work: An Anthology of Suffolk Stories* explores the varied forms of graft and labour that shape our county's past, present, and future. From our fishing and farming industries to the work of local communities in urban settings, towns and remote villages, these tales show how we are impacted by work in all its guises.

The stories in this collection speak of work that is fulfilling, challenging, liberating, or demoralising. From a village community fighting to save a local pub, to a young boy struggling to find his way in a quiet fishing hamlet, from an injured woman navigating a busy town market, to a seventeenth-century maker of bone lace, here are tales that illuminate, question, and playfully examine Freud's famous notion that all human life is concerned with love and work, and that's all there is.

Our anthology includes an introduction to each story, along with directions from our writers, so that you can visit every location as you read and reflect on what you find there. As an addition to the anthology, we have also included the winning, shortlisted, and longlisted entries from the Student New Angle Prize 2025, an award offered to students at the University of Suffolk by the Ipswich Institute, which runs the national *New Angle Prize* and the *Creative Suffolk Author Award*, sponsored by the University of Suffolk.

Many people have contributed to the work of this anthology. We would like to thank Dr Amanda Hodgkinson, Associate Professor in English and Creative Writing, for leading the production of this book. Thank you to our MA student, Amy Rehbein, for helping to edit and collate the collection, Jane Dixon-Smith for the book design and formatting, and Inge Shuster for the cover artwork. A special thank you to Ashley Hickson-Lovence, our Visiting Fellow in Creative Writing, novelist, poet, critic, and winner of the East Anglian Book of the Year 2024, for the foreword to the collection. Finally, a huge thank you and congratulations to our writers for their wonderful stories.

Dr Lindsey Scott
Senior Lecturer in English and MA Course Leader
University of Suffolk

Work

An Anthology of
Original Suffolk Stories

Foreword by award winning writer
Ashley Hickson-Lovence

F_33

F_16

F_92

Object_03V2

4583.76.453

First edition 2025

Published by the University of Suffolk Talking Shop Press,

Waterfront Building, 19 Neptune Quay, Ipswich IP4 1QJ

https://www.uos.ac.uk/courses/pg/ma-creative-and-critical-writing

Printed and bound in Great Britain by
Clays Ltd, Elcograf S.p.A
ISBN: 978-1-9989996-6-8

Introduction by Ashley Hickson-Lovence

"Work" is a word that underpins how we live, how we survive, how we create. And, when it comes to writing, work is not only part of the subject, it's embedded in the process itself. This anthology is a testament to both.

Every piece in this collection reflects the effort, the time, the concentration - the sheer commitment - that writing demands. But, when done well, it results in something lasting. And this collection stands as evidence of that. The contributors have brought their best and it shows. Because, make no mistake, writing takes work. From the initial spark of an idea to the final polish, it's a process that requires determination and discipline. There's the research, the planning, the drafting and redrafting. Then comes the editing - cutting, shaping, finessing - until the piece begins to resemble what the writer originally imagined. It can be slow, often challenging, but when done well, it's worth every hour. This anthology, filled with voices from across Suffolk, is proof of that.

As someone who works across different forms - from poetry and prose to performance - I know from first-hand experience how much time and energy goes into developing writing to a publishable standard. It's no small thing to produce work that's ready to be read by others. What you're holding in your hands is the product of that kind of effort: thoughtful, considered, crafted work that shines with clarity and care.

This is a collection that not only explores the idea of work, but also draws heavily on place. Each contribution is rooted in a specific location in Suffolk, and together they form a rich, textured portrait of the county. From Stowmarket to Southwold, Hadleigh to Hitcham - these writers offer windows into different lives and different labours, all set within landscapes that feel distinctly real and recognisably local.

The strength of this anthology lies in how it grounds the reader. The use of specific, named places gives each piece authenticity and depth. As a reader, you feel as though you're being guided through the streets, fields, factories and coastlines of Suffolk. These works are imagery-rich, yes, but not in a way that drifts into the inaccessible depths of the abstract. They are grounded. They are vivid. They are unapologetically real.

What you'll find here is a diverse range of writing - poetry and prose - that together paint a full and varied picture. The settings may shift, but the focus remains steady: on people, their work, and the places in which that work is done. The following pieces highlight the different rhythms and realities of working life. These are stories and poems that respect the routine as much as the extraordinary.

To readers: I encourage you to spend time with this collection. Let the stories and poems draw you in. Appreciate the precision of the language, the care in the construction, the respect for place. Allow yourself to travel - not just across the county, but into the minds and lives of the characters these writers have brought to life.

To the writers: your work here matters. The time you've invested, the decisions you've made, the moments of doubt you've pushed through - it's all led to something you should be proud of. This anthology is proof of all your hard work, your creativity, and your connection to both place and process.

This book is a celebration of writing, of Suffolk, and of the many forms that work can take.

Congratulations to all involved.

Dr. Ashley Hickson-Lovence
Fellow of Creative Writing
University of Suffolk

Contents

The National Horseracing Museum, Newmarket by Laura May

It feels like a gateway. As you drive into Newmarket along the A1304, green grass all around you, there is a crossing for the horses. It seems like a never-ending parade of warm breath, pure muscle and strength in each step. Only after you have paid this toll – witnessed this crossing – can you continue to the town of Newmarket and visit the National Horseracing Museum.

The National Horseracing Museum evolved from the building of Charles II's Newmarket Palace to the home of the Rothschild racing yard. Today, it traces the history of racing and British Sporting Art.

I was struck, as I took in the stories I found there, by just how many people work to make horseracing possible. I was particularly caught by the job of the farrier – highly skilled, patient, and vital. This inspired my poem, 'Farrier.'

Farrier

There's a care to be taken
when you lend a hand to heel, to heal.
My tools lick the edges of each wall
and my tongue clicks, shushes, soothes.

Do you remember the feel of wet barefoot mornings? Soft
shod
like a dancer lost in a slow tempo.
It doesn't matter now. You must be able to fly so
I scrape keratin against keratin – my fingernails – your
hoof –

nothing, my friend, will stop you in your tracks
I promise you, I am not here to break you, but to
be with you in stillness. There are no rider's hands here to
lean against –
just mine, at your service. Do you long for that time, as a
yearling,

before you tasted the bit and endlessly turned in circles,
a whirling dervish at the end of a long line,
or do you think only of now, as I bend your soles to my steel
so you can keep a man, a castle, that can fight?

No, I won't rush this.
Be still.
After all, my friend,
no hoof no horse.

Onehouse, Stowmarket by Noah Goldsworthy

St John the Baptist church stands on the foundations of a Saxon church in the village of Onehouse, Stowmarket. The building itself was said to have been rebuilt after the Norman conquest; archaeology has determined the oldest parts of the building are from the 1100s. The graves within the boundaries are multicentennial, with some as old as a month, others from the 1870s, and some belonging to a long-forgotten generation where no names are visible. St John the Baptist church was a part of parish group that managed the nearby workhouse from the late 1800s. The closest, a mere 1.4 miles away by road, was Stow Union Workhouse.

Now a private residential building, Stow Union Workhouse, originally bought for £1,200 in 1781, was a place people could go to get food and board in exchange for work. In the 1851 census, there were 225 inmates who lived, worked, and died within its walls. The workhouse had its own chapel. Since Christianity once saw poverty as a falling out of grace with God, paupers' graves were used to bury those who died within their walls. A mere iron number plate was placed on a wooden cross to mark their shallow resting place. The paupers' graves have been kept by volunteers since the 2000s. Now, a plaque with the names of all those who died at the workhouse between 1813 and 1835 stands by the entrance of the graves.

I was inspired to write about these three places because, in my culture, people only truly die when they are no longer spoken about. I believe it is the duty of every generation to pass on the stories of our ancestors. Of course, my piece is fiction through and through; it was unheard of for an inmate of a workhouse to share a church pew with the higher class of society. However, I wanted to engage people in the humanity of a story, without class barriers, to question their own perception of what is important. That included complex questioning of John's own faith in following men's rules. With the very earth yearning for him to stop digging, he finally makes an unapologetic decision and does the human thing. Instead of burying Emily on her own under the bushes, he buries her with her parents.

Inmate 61

Paul Stannard, the sexton of St John the Baptist, was standing by the church door unloading his grave-digging tools from his cart to his wheelbarrow. The snow had fallen for four days in a row and barely any of the stained glass of the eastern wall could be made out. A thick sheet had covered the houses, fields, and workhouse. The graves at St John the Baptist could barely be seen until you were within the grounds of the churchyard.

It was Thursday 7 January 1897 and, as the sun began to rise, Paul was planning to dig a grave for Inmate 61 from the workhouse. Today was the day Paul Stannard would break the law of man and stand steadfast to the law of God.

The breath from my mouth interrupted my eyes as it lingered in front of my face. I walked towards the edge of the churchyard with the stakes and yarn to mark out the grave. My feet sunk into the snow with each fresh footprint. I could hear the *shhh* and feel the crunch under my boots. Nearby, I spotted the tracks of a mouse making its way towards the field. Fox prints and a nose-shaped scoop in the snow shortly followed.

I tried to push the first stake into the ground by hand, but it was frozen solid. I grabbed a large rock from under the bushes and was able to break into the earth. I did the same with three other stakes, then wrapped the yarn to mark out where I would be digging. I measured the rectangle to make sure it was going to be big enough. I put a few potato sacks on the snow next to it.

Then I heard someone walking in the snow.

'Who's there?'

'Are ya right, buh?' My brother, Luke, emerged from the side of the church carrying a small coffin and two spades. 'Cold mornin' int it?'

'Too, right,' I said, pointing to the side of the rectangle. 'Pop it there, buh.'

I watched as Luke dodged the gravestones and placed the small coffin on top of the potato sacks. He handed me one of the spades.

We started to pile the snow under the bushes. We tried cutting into the earth but, as with the stakes, it was frozen. We carried on slamming the blades until the ground gave up its integrity. Then we began cutting squares of grass. They came up as stiff as the corpses we put in the graves. The ground was a thick and heavy clay that I'd not come across here before. It would take time to settle when refilled. *Her parents' grave was a pleasure to dig. A few tree roots, but nothing difficult.*

Luckily, there were no tree roots to cut. I'd forgotten my saw.

Luke had gone back to his wife and children. I was there by myself. The grave continued to be difficult. A frozen top layer, thick and heavy clay, and now I had to bail out water three times. It was only three feet deep, but I had to keep pushing back the walls so they didn't fall in on me. I'd been digging for almost two hours. My hands were burning as my tools had torn some of the calluses off my palm. My lips were numb, I could barely speak, and I had clay in my eyes. But finally, I had completed my task. I climbed up my short ladder and out of the grave. I turned to look at the sun which made the snow sparkle like diamonds. Then I spotted a group of men, led by Matthew, walking across the glistening field. Watching them, I could feel a sharp breeze picking up.

I walked back to my cart and loaded my wheelbarrow with all the sackcloth I had brought, planks of wood and two lengths of rope. On the way back to the grave, my wheelbarrow knocked into the graves of Sarah and Albert Jennings, Emily's parents. The planks scattered on the floor and the sackcloth started blowing away with the wind. I quickly gathered them up and made my way to the grave I had dug outside the church's boarders. I cautiously dropped planks around the edges of the grave, being careful not to make the walls cave in. I waited for a few moments, listening to the earth whine and creek under the weight of the planks.

As Matthew came closer, I could see that he was carrying his cousin, Emily. She was in a white dress, laying stiff across his arms. I couldn't help but stare at her. *She's so thin.* My mind drifted back to a time when I had to tell her off, and my own daughters, for misbehaving in the pews behind. That was before she was forced into the workhouse.

The men with Matthew took off the lid of the coffin and Matthew placed her inside. She looked like an angel. My breath caught as the walls of the grave suddenly began to collapse. At the same time, the holy spirit ignited something inside me.

I can't do this.

'She must be laid to rest next to her parents, as it should be!' My words echoed through the silence and the lump in my throat subsided. 'These are the rules of man, not God.

If a girl like that can lose favour with God because of her circumstances, then I want no part of it.'

The men from the workhouse stared at me, then nodded. One by one, they stepped over the threshold and started digging a new grave for Emily beside her parents. The soil wasn't frozen by Sarah and Albert. There were no roots to be cut, no water to be bailed.

After the funeral, Matthew lay the final piece of grass. A Hawfinch perched on the handle of the shovel, watching. Matthew looked at the finch and I heard him whisper.

'Fly away, little cousin. You're free now.'

The Food Museum, Stowmarket by Amy Rehbein

The Food Museum in Stowmarket, formally known as The Museum of East Anglian Life, is embedded in my family history. My grandad helped to set up the museum for its opening in 1967, while my nan, mum, aunties, and uncle all volunteered at the museum at different stages throughout their lives.

Despite having some setbacks in his life, my grandad never lost his passion for farming and carried on pursuing this passion until he could no longer do so. My inspiration for this story, 'Echoes of the Past,' stems both from my Suffolk farming heritage and my eight-year-old niece, Tilly, and her fascination with the 'olden days.' Bringing these two ideas together took me on an emotional journey of personal discovery, loss, and love.

To get to The Food Museum, come off the A14 at Junction 50 and follow the A1120 to Stowmarket. The museum is located on Iliffe Way, near to the Asda car park.

In loving memory of Brian George Rush, 1940 – 2015.

Echoes of the Past

Lily ran into the museum at full steam, leaving her parents trailing behind.

'Come on!' she called, almost running past the main desk, knowing that just around the corner, a whole world was waiting to be discovered. The *olden days*, that's what people called the past. To Lily, this was an adventure she had chosen especially to celebrate her eighth birthday.

Lily's first-ever visit to The Food Museum was extra special. She'd heard stories from her parents of how her great grandad had helped to set up the museum. Back in 1967, it had been known as The Museum of East Anglian Life. To Lily, 1967 sounded like a different world. She often thought that if she had a time machine, she'd love to go back and visit that time to see what it was truly like. Her great nanny had shown her photos of herself and her great grandad growing up in that time, but to experience it in person would have been much better.

Lily wanted to discover what her great grandad had done in the past. She'd heard from her great nanny that despite him losing his right arm at the age of fifteen, he'd never given up on his dream of working on Suffolk farms. He'd eventually achieved that dream at the age of twenty, working at Chapels Farm in Stowupland. Lily didn't know how her great grandad lost his arm. She'd never been told, but she'd heard the words *shooting* and *accident* in conversations that took place behind closed doors. *How could you do work with one arm?* she wondered. She could only imagine that it took a lot of practice and patience. It made her admire her great grandad even more.

'Ready to go?' her mum asked, stepping away from the main desk. 'I thought we could visit the Medieval Barn first.'

Lily nodded and ran off, eager to begin her adventure.

The sheer size of the barn, with its large doors, two floors, and sturdy structure made entirely of wood and brick was unlike anything Lily had ever seen before.

'This barn was first used between the 13th and 15th century and has had repairs to keep it in shape,' her dad explained, walking along beside her.

Somewhere inside Lily's head, a light switched on. 'That's not just the olden days, Daddy,' she said. 'That's the olden, olden, *olden* days.'

Lily wanted to learn more. She'd never been anywhere that was this old. She didn't even think her great nanny would know anything about such a faraway time, and that was saying something. Great Nanny knew the answer to every question Lily asked.

Lily's small hands stroked every surface she could find. Her eyes roamed every nook and cranny, not wanting to miss a single detail. She felt the roughness of the wooden structure holding the barn together, the bumpy texture underneath her hands. The dry, mealy smell of straw and grain hit her nostrils. This smell alone transported her back in time.

She started to imagine the sound of the workers talking to each other as they unloaded wagons full of harvested crops and carried them to the second floor to be processed. The sound would probably be deafening, and in response, Lily covered her ears. She could feel the draughts of cold

air that would come through the small cracks in the doors, and she shivered slightly.

'Lily, come and look at this,' her dad called, snapping her out of her time travelling. He was standing in front of a display of photographs.

Lily wandered over and looked at a particular photograph closely, studying every detail. The picture was black and white. In it, a group of farm workers stood together with huge forks and shovels in their hands. The workers wore flat caps, welly boots, dark trousers and shirts. Lily noticed a strange-looking machine in the background. It was enormous with big wheels and moving parts that looked shiny, even in black and white. Lily tried to imagine it working, but all she could see in her mind was a tangled mess of gears and metal.

'It's called a Thresher,' her dad said. 'Farm workers used it to separate grain seeds from stalks and husks. Your great grandad used to use one of these on the farms. I believe he used to work on repairing the threshing drums, too.'

Lily continued to examine the photograph. *Did the farmers have fun using the thresher? Was it hard work? What happened if it started raining?*

Amid these thoughts, she saw a man standing behind her. A man with one arm.

Her great grandad.

Lily recognised him instantly. She'd seen enough photos to know what he looked like. *What was he doing here, though?* He was meant to be in heaven.

'Oh Lily,' he said with a broad Suffolk accent, looking straight at her. 'If only you knew the work that went into threshing. For us farm workers, it was a demanding job.' He paused, staring at the photograph. Lily watched him with awe.

'Why?' she asked, wondering if he would hear her. His next words told her that he could.

'Well, for one, the long hours. Threshing happened during the harvest season when demand was critical. It felt like you were living only to work at points. We would leave, go home, sleep, get up early, and then do it all over again.' A long sigh escaped his lips.

'That *does* sound demanding,' said Lily, letting out a little sigh of her own.

'Not to mention physically exhausting,' said her great grandad. 'The job was draining. You needed strength, you needed grit, and you needed to be on the move constantly. Lifting the sheaves of grain into the machine and dealing with heavy bundles of straw with my one arm was harder for me than most. I remember one time almost passing out under the late August sun. So, Lily, my sweet girl, this job was tough. Tougher than you could ever imagine.'

Lily watched as her great grandad smiled and walked out of the barn. She was about to follow him when her mum and dad each took one of her hands.

'We want to show you something,' Mum said. She smiled and followed Great Grandad's footsteps without even knowing he was there.

They ended up at another building called *Mortlock*.

What a strange name, Lily thought as she entered the building. After a few more steps, she came face to face with a large machine that had huge wheels made of shiny black metal. A series of pipes and levers gleamed. At the front of the machine, a long silver nozzle stuck up into the air. Lily instantly wanted to know what that was used for.

'It's called a traction engine,' her dad explained, leaning over her shoulder. 'Your great grandad used to look after these. He even had one in the front garden of his house at one point.'

Lily grinned. She moved around the building, looking for her great grandad again. She wanted to know what the machines were used for and hoped he would explain. As if he could read her mind, he appeared beside her.

'Traction engines,' he said with a wink. 'My passion. I put so much work into repairing these things. I miss them even now.'

Lily listened, trying to imagine what it must be like to miss a machine.

'They were vital for our works on the farms, my dear. Some were opposed to using them. See, there was a time when machines like this weren't around. I, for one, welcomed the change. They helped power our threshing machine using steam, making the work slightly easier. My love and passion for them continued, and you may have heard stories of me having one in my front garden! I used to run it from time to time, and all the neighbours would come out and have a look.'

'Lily!' Mum called from the other side of the building, where she and Dad were waiting. 'Let's go and look at something else. Time is ticking on.'

'Time is certainly ticking on, Lily,' said her great grandad. 'Make sure you cherish every minute.'

Lily nodded in agreement, then reluctantly walked away. Taking her parents' hands, she stepped out into the open. The fresh dewy smell of spring hit her nostrils and rays from the sun dazzled her eyes.

Taking one last look behind, she saw her great grandad waving as he drifted into the sunlight. She desperately wanted him to stay, but she knew in her heart that he couldn't. As for her, she had to carry on with her own adventures. She had a whole future ahead.

Hitcham by Sheena McCallum

This story is set in Hitcham, a very rural village stretched over three miles in southern Suffolk, on the road that runs north from Hadleigh to Stowmarket.

Inevitably, one's feelings about a location are determined not just by its characteristics and those that live there, but also by one's own circumstances and view of life at that time – a diplomatic way of saying that I hated Hitcham and haven't been back since 1988.

However, I was a teenager (I lived there from age twelve to eighteen) and teenagers aren't known for their love of rural locations, unrenovated cottages, a lack of like-minded teenagers, an absence of public transport, or anywhere other than *the bench* to hang out (if they had anyone to hang out with).

Having wracked my brain very hard, I can recall some positives to life in Hitcham. The kindness of a true local who baked us a chocolate cake and gave us eggs every week when funds were low. The freedom to roam and play in both our garden and the common plots and open fields beyond. The booming jets and unexpected Red Arrow displays from RAF Wattisham, which provided the odd jolt of excitement. The pretty, renovated cottages owned by other people.

The characters in this story are based on my brothers and me, and the story is largely true, although it merges two separate events. The mood of the story reflects my memories of the village, but I'm happy to say my brothers and I get on much better as adults!

Siblings

The November fog showed no sign of lifting. Emma could only just see the outline of the hedgerow at the far end of the sloping field. There was no hint of the village, Hitcham, beyond. The world was reduced to monochrome; the cloud, silhouettes of bare oak trees, the wet, dark Suffolk soil and the farmyard. Only the creamy yellow skins of potatoes protruding from the soil and the coats of the small workforce, collecting them by hand, injected any sense of colour.

Emma looked over her shoulder, having filled her first crate of the day and wanting to gauge how well the boys were doing. Or, more to the point, how much money they'd earned so far. The problem with being paid by the crate was that she was taking home £4 a day for completing two crates, whereas her younger brothers and their four friends, who were pooling their efforts, were making about £8 a day each. They wouldn't let her join them because, as they repeatedly told her, *she was an annoying girl and much slower than they were*.

Simon, her youngest brother, spotted her looking over.

'What's up, slowcoach?'

'Shut up, will you?' said Emma, pulling off her Mum's slightly too big gardening gloves to rub her frozen fingers together. She made a mental note not to forget her own woolly gloves to put on underneath tomorrow.

Simon ignored her and she moved away from the boys and across to the next row so that she could begin filling her

19

second crate. No one had started on the row yet and potatoes stretched ahead in a meandering line that disappeared into the foggy gloom. She bent over and wrapped her glove around the closest one, instantly feeling the damp and cold through the cloth. Heavy clay soil clung to each potato. In drier weather, it might have been possible to lift each potato cleanly out of the ground, but in early November, each one stuck to the clay. She used her other hand to knock off the worst. She recoiled as a fat, grey-mauve earthworm fell to the ground with the soil. Worms had repulsed her since she was tiny. She squirmed as she reached over to the new crate to drop the potato in. The wooden crate was three feet square and she was determined to fill it before the end of the day. She had to work fast, otherwise the farmer would insist on working out the exact value of a not-quite-full crate. The day before, Emma had been reprimanded by the farm worker in charge for leaving too much mud on the potatoes and was filling her crates even more slowly now that she had to stop and remove as much as she could.

Emma's thoughts turned, as they had all week, to how else she might earn money. There had to be something better than picking up potatoes in cold fog whilst trying to avoid the repugnant, wriggling inhabitants of the soil. She stretched upwards and pushed her shoulders down, trying to relieve the pressure on her back and thought again about beating with the shoot. But the idea of guiding pheasants and partridges to their death and picking them up afterwards remained even worse than the potatoes.

There had to be something else – babysitting perhaps? If she could find a family who needed someone. Or cutting grass for elderly people?

All she needed was enough money to buy some decent clothes so she could fit in with the other girls from school. Homemade clothes didn't work when you were fourteen. She'd had enough of the jokes and teasing.

Emma tried to focus and inched her way along the line, bending over repeatedly to pick up each potato. She knocked a just-about-acceptable amount of mud off each before putting it in the canvas bag tied around her waist. Then she returned to the crate to empty the small bag of around ten potatoes. The distance back to the crate kept increasing the further along the row she got, and consequently, the rate at which she filled the crate became slower and slower.

The afternoon passed interminably slowly and her back became more and more sore. She could feel the cold being conducted into her body through the soles of her wellies, as light in the sky began to fade. Emma tried to focus instead on her forthcoming shopping trip with Justine. She hoped to have earned £20 by Friday, the final day of both half term and potato picking. On Saturday, they were going to get the bus from Bildeston into Ipswich and spend the afternoon shopping. Justine had painted a vivid image of a Clock-house black-and-white striped shirt in a shiny material that she had seen in C&A, and the racks of bright, colourful clothes in Chelsea Girl were sure to offer up some gems. Emma was desperate to buy some bright leggings and a baggy shirt before the next football club disco.

A voice broke her thoughts and she looked up through the damp fog to see her other brother standing over her.

'Oi, Emma! I swear you get slower every single day. You still not finished?'

It was Colin, the middle sibling. He knew better than anyone else in the world how to wind her up. Especially when there was a captive audience of his two friends, plus Simon and the younger boys. There they stood, in a halo of mist, looking down at her as she stooped over in the mud.

Emma swore quietly to herself. Yet again, they'd finished and would have twice the money she had. She looked to the cold mud. Bending down, she picked up a large potato and then another, sidestepping a large worm with a nonchalance she didn't feel.

'Oi, Emma, are you deaf, as well as fat and slow?'

Emma glared at him. Colin lowered his arm, and she felt something disgusting hit the side of her cheek.

'What was that?' she started, before realising that whatever it was, it was now stuck in her long, wavy hair. She pulled furiously at the strands with her gloved hand and a vile, slithery worm fell onto the soil. Emma stared at it as it writhed on the ground. She thought she might throw up.

She screamed at Colin. 'You idiot! What the hell? You're … a … *fucking cunt!*'

She froze, horrified, cheeks flaming, as a cold sweat began to spread through her body. Everyone was looking at her. The boys, the two farm workers, and the handful of older villagers also helping had all stopped what they were doing. Emma bit her lip, trying to stop the tears pricking behind her eyes. She had no idea where those forbidden words had come from.

'Whoaa! Oh, my God! It was only a worm,' said Colin. His eyes lit up and he erupted into laughter. 'Wait until I tell Mum and Dad. Simon, did you hear what she actually said?'

'Yeah, unbelievable from Miss Goody-two-shoes!' Simon replied.

Emma turned away from them and walked slowly across to her still-not-full crate. 'Don't say anything. Don't tell Mum and Dad. Please,' she implored, turning back to Colin with tears rolling down her cheeks.

The other workers had returned to their work, but Colin stood still, his hands on his hips. He looked to the potato crate. 'Give me your money from today,' he said. 'If you give it to me, I won't say anything to Mum and Dad.'

'What about me?' Simon piped up. 'She needs me to stay quiet, too!'

'Okay, you get £1 and I get £3.'

'Seriously? You're *blackmailing* me?' Emma stared at Colin in disbelief, a large potato in her hands. She waved it at him furiously. 'First you throw a worm in my face and now you want my money? The money it took me all day to earn?'

'Yep, looks like it,' said Colin, turning on his heel and marching off down the track.

Emma watched him go, his band of followers in tow behind. As she stood there, her fury transformed into a burning desire for justice. She was the one who had worked for this money and *she was the one who was going to keep it*. After all, he wouldn't ever dare repeat those words to their parents. Her mind flashed forward to Saturday, and the clothes sat waiting in town.

'Okay, tell them, then,' she shouted after him. 'There's no way in hell that you're taking my money!'

Hadleigh by Harry Searle

Being from an 'army family,' I moved around a lot in my younger years, in and out of the country. Since settling in Suffolk almost fifteen years ago, Hadleigh has become as close to a hometown as I've known. So, when I was set the task of producing a piece of writing for this anthology, it seemed appropriate to dedicate it to the town in which I was fortunate enough to spend much of my teenage years.

Upon research, it came as a pleasant surprise that (as somebody with an interest in history), I found that Hadleigh has had a varied past, from a Viking King and the Peasants' Revolt to the persecution (and subsequent burning) of Protestants under the reign of Queen Mary I. Fascinating stuff, but as anybody who lives there now will perhaps know, Hadleigh is mostly regarded for its agricultural background, which my poem, 'Fieldworkers,' explores.

Aiming to capture the gruelling slog of rural farmwork in the mid-Victorian era, the poem is not necessarily based upon one particular locale in the town. Instead, it draws upon the ancient and worked land Hadleigh sits upon – walk across any of the fields surrounding the town and the spire of St Mary's church will eventually loom into view, much the same as it did for those that worked the local fields in years long past.

Fieldworkers

Hadleigh, Suffolk, 1850

Working through the day, until quiet dusk.
Ceaseless toil under the burning of the sun,
Skin cracked and muddied, a sallow husk.
Dig stone from the clog while the show-sheep run
Freely from the butcher's bloody knife,
Toward the end of their days; unknown of the life
Lived by all of us simple things. Axes held
Two-handed, firm, deep in thought. *Nay!*
Splintered tools, and the fleeches fray,
Gathering wood from yonder trees felled.

Alas! Pocketing a turnip for 'morrow's stew,
Lest the wage be delayed or variously gant.
Spying the daw above, away sunward it flew;
Sole witness to the root-theft, signals with its chant.
Now return to the work, tool – crusted and foul.
Unsheath the earth with shovel, pick, trowel,
Belonging among it all; retrieve the crop
Through twist and pull – toss into the ratty sack.
What bounty given forth! Carted down the track
To the plates of better, elvish men, of milksop.

Benumbing thoughts from elite stares. Not pity,
Fear almost. It twinkles from behind their eyes
Upon retreat with purchase to safeties of smogged city,
Recalling fairytales of the raiders 'neath holy skies
Rued with history, standing tall – yet the past
Is sunk into the mud now tilled, separating caste.
Come down off your carriage and dig!
Join in the maggot and the louse and squirm
Among the flea, the beetle and the worm,
In place of the gold, the jewel, the powdered whig.

The slog marches. Fan the horse that ploughs!
Drive onward, beast, you cease when told.
Unfasten the darnel and drake as strength allows!
St Mary rings midday; devilish sun, gazing bold.
Sweat dribbles and runs from many a furrowed brow,
Cutting lines in caked dust and grime of faces now
grim and gaunt. Rest not, for here these wages
Are for labourers, not shiftless folk – but then,
A rallying cry! *We worked before, we'll work again!*
Ho! Our slumber tonight will be one for the ages!

At last! Ambling through the town, cheerily weary,
Past church, past old king's ghost – left behind.
A look of contempt across all, though leary
Of the next day unless rain should fall, divined.
Let the water wash away the toil and evince
The scant faces of these who work ever since.
They stow away tools and bathe calloused hands,
Returning now to homes and simple comfort
In those four walls – all kings of the court.
Last they sleep, with wishful dreams of faraway lands.

Flatford by Jessica Spence

Work is a difficult concept to contextualise. However, in writing this story, I was inspired by my fascination of the human body and how hard life can be. My intention was to show that the scope of the word 'work' is not as limited as we might think it is. My story is set in the rolling fields of Flatford Mill. I hope it gives you a new perspective on work and what it can mean.

Living Life

Define what the word 'work' means to you. How do you come to this conclusion and why?

I have lost count of how many times I have stared at that question in growing frustration in the past four hours. I slam my laptop lid down. *Of all the questions, why is this one so hard?*

I would have already given up, but this was the writing opportunity of a lifetime for me. I couldn't just quit. I heave a sigh of frustration. I'm getting nowhere. *Maybe a walk will do me some good?*

Snatching my backpack from the bed, I stomp down the stairs, hoping to find Mum.

I enter the kitchen where I bang and bash about, filling my metal water bottle, sliding a banana into my bag and checking what I need.

The living room door swings open and Mum enters the hallway.

'Everything OK?' she asks.

'Yeah,' I say. 'I'm gonna walk to Flatford. Shall I meet you there?' I grab my hiking boots, sitting on the stairs to lace them up. Mum is stood before me.

'Writing trouble?'

I look her dead. *How does she always know?* I nod stiffly. She smiles and I feel just a bit calmer.

'Have you got a drink, your inhaler?'

'Yes, Mum.' I spring to my feet and quickly kiss her on the cheek.

'Meet me at the café at 1pm!' she calls. I wave to acknowledge as she follows me to the door.

'Love you.'

I close the passage door with a grin. I'm not expecting a reply. She already told me with her smile. I heave a sigh, leave the front drive and begin my walk, thoughts muddling over my problem.

Work. The very word makes my blood boil. It travels to the hours of my life I currently spend pouring over job applications. The nagging and endless thoughts of money and self-doubt. Never achieving anything, never amounting to anything. *Can't do it, you don't cut it.* Over and over, friends and family badger you, demanding you do more. *Why can't you get a job? It's not that hard.*

The road turns into the dirt tracks of the public footpaths. I keep up a fast pace, burning through my frustration. The green landscape narrows before widening into fields. Panting softly, I find myself sitting on the first bench I find. Anger extinguished.

I lose track of how long I sit there, breathing in the floral grassy scent. Bees and birds pass in and out of my vision, whizzing back and forth to complete their tasks for the day.

I wish I could stay forever, watching the endless grassy plains, listening to the swans and ducks yapping in the nearby marshland as they feed their young. The faint sounds of domestic wildlife mixing in with the wild.

But I need to keep walking.

As I trudge the path, I hear the faint echo of the train. I wonder whether it was Liverpool Street to Norfolk, or the opposite. The walk to Flatford expands to wide meadows, bordered by hedgerow that closes them into sections. Livestock gets moved via gates across these meadows and people via a little double-gated circle mechanism. It always makes me smile going through them. In one way, you push the gate forward, then land in the big circle, and swing the gate to behind as you go out.

As I walk, I pass fields devoid of mammals, then others full of the wildlife of England. Rabbits and sheep grazing, unbothered by my presence.

The green visions of nature lull my mind. My body feels softly heavier as I plod down the trail. I am no closer to my answer. *Define what the word 'work' means to you.* An itch in my mind drives me back to the bees. Bees and work, there's something there. It's on the tip of my tongue.

Adjusting my straps to ward off a sudden mild discomfort in my chest, I try to push the bees from my mind and focus on ahead. Ahead. Where a closed gate stands. I catch the sign on the gate. It's not often Flatford or the paths through the fields close a gate.

No unleashed dogs past this point.
Ewes and lambs are grazing in this field.
Failure to comply will result in penalty under...

I skip the punishment and legislation jargon. I don't have a dog, so it doesn't concern me. But the second line does. *Lambs.* It's not often you get to see lambs in the public fields.

Hopping over the gate, I'm greeted by a scene I can only describe as joy. There's no other way to describe a field full of ewes with their lambs. Bleating and twittering, they merge into nature's orchestra. The lambs are like little white clouds, darting back and forth around the patiently watching ewes. Lambs are chasing one another, jumping, rolling. I try to smile but now my chest hurts. I check my watch. 12.36pm.

Better get a move on or I won't get to the mill by 1pm.
I follow the footpath as it skirts around the edge of the

field. My chest pain stabs low in my ribs. Blood pumps loudly in my ears. I raise my hand as the world falls mute.

I can't breathe.

Adrenaline pumps fast into me. Pulling my backpack open, I fumble with the zip. My chest feels like 1000 needles as I reach into my bag. My vision blurs but I don't need sight. The smooth plastic is a familiar shape in my palm. I drop to my knees. Wrenching the inhaler from the bag, I shove the end into my mouth. My teeth ache. I push the presser.

My hearing latches onto the noise. I feel it in my throat. I try to breathe. I order everything in my body to obey. My lungs rattle as I take in a breath.

Slowly, my vision expands from its tunnel and each breath feels sweet to my stale tongue. I can feel every part of me again. Every twitch of limb, every pulsing organ as they push through nerve signals to work. To thrive, to survive, to live. It feels more of an effort than the hardest working day. The work of needing to live.

My hands grip the grass before me, dirt digging into my nails. Breathing aches and my bones feel like stone as I stretch my back, expanding my lungs.

The world returns to me with a quiet bleat. Raising my head, I come face to face with a lamb. Knobbly legs shaking, spine hunched in, eyes staring at me intently. I realise then that the lamb looks exhausted. Its white wool is splashed with mud and it's shivering. I can't help but feel some kindred spirit with this curious little creature.

Hobbling, it approaches before slowly folding to rest, placing its head near my knees. I can feel the lamb's warmth. I'm sure it can feel mine. I glance around for its mother. With a shaky hand, I take another puff of my inhaler and stare at the lamb. My hand stretches to its head, feeling the soft wool.

We both just sit there, working on staying alive. There we are, me and the lamb, and this day where the sun shines and there are bees, and the ground is damp underneath me. I realise then that this is the answer to my question.

Once I gain the strength, I collect my backpack and the lamb, then head for the mill. I pass the lamb to one of the workers, who promises to get it looked at.

Mum is already at the café. Taking one look at me, it's clear that she knows what's just happened. You can't hide anything from a nurse.

Mum sets me down at a table by the large window that opens onto the river Stour. Just in front of the bank, ducks mill about in the water. I hang my backpack on the wooden chair and grab the notebook and pen lurking in the bottom. My mind is full of ideas as my pen hits the page.

Mum comes to the table with a tray of drinks. She taps my shoulder as she sits down, looking at my notebook.

'Did you get what you needed?'

My gaze turns to the river, a smile clinging to my lips. 'Yeah.'

The word feels warm in my heart.

Somersham by Ben Collins

The Duke of Marlborough is one of several community-owned pubs in Suffolk. Although it lies on the periphery of the village of Somersham, it is very much at the heart of the community. In a time where all too many of us live in our bubbles, it is a place where everyone, from four-year-old Ruby to ninety-year-old Denis can nod their heads at each other and exchange a few words. And it would have been lost to the village forever, had it not been for the tireless efforts and boundless optimism of a group of villagers who were determined not to let it go. Theirs was a labour of love. Sadly, the work is still not done, for in these straightened times, the pub fights on for its survival from week to week. So, come, raise a glass, and join the cause!

The Volunteer

When the email landed in his inbox, Steve was busy Googling his symptoms. His doctor said that his chest pains were caused by anxiety, but he wasn't convinced. The alternative diagnoses offered by the search engine, however, were making his chest tighten more than ever. He was grateful for the distraction offered by the incoming message.

Disappointingly, it proved to be more junk from *MyNeighbour.com*. It irritated him that Eluned had signed them up to the site in the first place. It was supposed to be a 'community space' where local news and events could be posted. In his opinion, it seemed to be a forum for griping about life's trifles.

He scanned the subject line without optimism.

'The Duke needs *you!*' it declared.

Steve was surprised to find his curiosity pricked.

The Duke. He hadn't given the pub a thought in ages.

Once upon a time, he'd been the regular's regular, sinking the pints, playing darts, chewing the fat. Then the landlord had changed and his best pint had been taken off. Work picked up, Eluned got sick, and without ever meaning to, he'd got out of the habit of going. Next thing he'd heard, the place had folded and for the first time in 500 years, Somersham was without a drinking hole. The news was sad, of course, but back then, he'd had more pressing preoccupations.

He clicked on the link inserted in the message and brought up the post. A photo of a crowd of cheering people waving banners and pint glasses filled the top of the screen. Steve's gaze skated over the sea of smiling faces down to the write-up.

'The Duke of Marlborough has been saved for the community,' it trumpeted. 'After two years of fundraising, we have finally taken possession of the keys to this iconic building. But now the *real* work begins. After years of standing empty, *your* pub is in urgent need of some TLC. Can you spare some time to come and help out this Saturday? We need ...'

Two years – had it really been that long?

Steve returned his gaze to the celebrating villagers and tried to pick out any faces he knew. For some reason, though, his eyes couldn't focus. He rubbed them with the back of one hand and massaged his chest with the other and clicked off the site. *Good luck to them.* The pub was part of the past and there was no going back there. He stood abruptly and headed to the kitchen to fix some dinner.

The doorbell chimed while he was stabbing indifferently at a plate of food in front of the box. Surprised to have a visitor late on a Friday, he poked his head out the front door, expecting to see yet another errant delivery driver.

'Stevo!' boomed a voice in greeting.

There was no mistaking that voice. It was Frank. Frank had been one of his best drinking buddies, but without the pub to anchor them, they'd drifted.

'Oh, alright there, Frank. Long time no see. What's up?' Steve frowned. It wasn't like Frank to call around out of the blue.

'I wanted to see if I could persuade you to come out tomorrow. To help at The Duke.'

So that was it: he'd come on the cadge. Come to think of it, the last time Steve saw Frank was when he was selling him raffle tickets in support of the pub.

'I dunno,' he mumbled. 'I'm not feeling too good at the moment. Been off work.'

'Mate, I'm sorry to hear that,' replied Frank, looking genuinely crestfallen. 'Nothing serious, I hope?'

Steve shrugged. He didn't like to talk about illness.

'Well, it'd be great to see you up there. For old times' sake, eh? I won't hold you to wielding a paint brush.'

'I'll see,' said Steve noncommittally.

He closed the door, but Steve found that he couldn't get The Duke out of his head. He grubbed around in the dresser for the photo albums and found himself entertained for the rest of the evening with memories of trendy haircuts and youthful faces (Eluned really had been a cracker back then) crowded in the bar. It was strange to think that he hadn't set eyes on the place in months. His route to work took him the other way out of the village and he'd not had cause to go anywhere else.

Perhaps, he thought, *I'll take a wander that way tomorrow. It'll do me good to get some fresh air, and anything's got to be better than sitting around here not working.*

The following morning, Steve stood on the pavement opposite the pub. It wasn't a promising scene. The paint was peeling. Weeds had taken over the car park. Even the old sign had gone missing. He wished he hadn't come. The happy memories that had filled his head the day before were starting to tarnish. He turned to walk away.

A sharp whistle and a shout of 'Hey, Stevo!' caused him to pause. It was Frank – he was poking his head out of the pub's main entrance and waving.

'I knew you wouldn't be able to keep away! Come in and say hello.'

Suddenly, there were the chest pains again. Steve gritted his teeth in discomfort. He felt like running away but that, he knew, would look ridiculous. Besides, Frank was already crossing the road towards him, looking concerned.

'You OK?' he asked.

'Yeah. Just a bit of heartburn.'

Steve let himself be led into the pub with a friendly arm around his shoulder. Frank explained enthusiastically what was planned. Inside, they found several people propping up the bar. Three of them, Steve knew; the fourth face was unfamiliar.

'This is Joan,' said Frank, making the introduction. 'She lives a few doors down from you.'

That was news to Steve. He couldn't recall having set eyes on her before and there would be no missing her in a hurry; of that, he was certain. In the drab interior of the pub, she stood out, a vibrant pop of colour with her curly red bob and bright pink blouse.

'I'm the red Toyota and the gnomes,' said Joan with a smile.

'I'm the silver Renault and the brick weave,' said Steve, his mouth stretching into an involuntary grin.

Just like that, his tongue was away. He hadn't had a proper conversation with anyone in ages. The knot of tension in between his shoulders steadily relaxed as his earlier misgivings about venturing over the threshold ebbed away. It was only when more volunteers joined and Frank began to organise his troops that Steve recalled the purpose of the gathering.

'OK, everyone,' Frank called, evidently enjoying himself. 'Let's do some work!'

Steve soon found himself with Joan in the dingy yellow

walled snug sniggering over a tin of emulsion – the pub committee had settled on a trendy muted colour palette, which neither of them found appealing. Even so, after a few passes of his roller, Steve had to admit that the cool grey freshened the space immeasurably.

It occurred to him that the last time he had stood in the room, he'd been half-cut and sounding off about Town's current form to anyone who would listen. If he was being honest with himself, he was having a much better time now.

Who'd have thought, he marvelled to himself, *that you could have more fun in a pub with paint than a pint?*

When a halt was called to their collective labours at midday, Steve was disappointed that the time had passed so quickly. The thought of returning home to sit alone was distinctly unappealing.

'Will we see you again next Saturday?' asked Frank at the door. 'We've still got a lot of work to do here.'

Steve looked over Frank's shoulder to where Joan was busy folding some dustsheets. She stood in vivid contrast to the newly painted walls. When she looked up, she flashed him a smile. Steve flashed one back, and for the first time, he sensed Eluned's ghost fading a little. A feeling of peace unfurled in his chest.

He nodded at Frank.

'Saturday,' he said. 'I'll see.'

Ipswich by Roy Haddock

Good stories are handed from generation to generation. This story, set in Ipswich during the 1960s when the firm Ransome Simms and Jeffries was at its peak, tells the tale of my grandad and an incident in his life that highlights the changes in employment law and society he and his colleagues fought for. Each generation often forgets the sacrifices of the last. Family history may be recounted without any real understanding of the suffering endured. This story has been recounted, laughed at, and debated around many a Sunday dinner table.

The Emperor's New Clothes

The clock on the mantlepiece chimed nine. William stared into the mirror above whilst warming his legs by the fire. The eyes that stared back had lost their sparkle. Studying the lines on his face, he contemplated each one, chiselled by hardship and graft. Time had not been kind. He felt old, a feeling that had become common.

In the corner of the reflection was his loving, enduring wife Margaret, sitting on a threadbare sofa. She brushed the shoulders of his old jacket. He picked up the letter from behind the clock. He didn't understand why he had received it, but there it was in black and white.

In Reward for Loyal Service.

He was to be taken to Coe's Outfitters to receive a new wardrobe of clothes. Anything he desired, apparently. The works manager had quoted him to be the equivalent of *Ransome Royalty*. The main thing was that it had made Margaret happy.

'William Haddock!' she called from the sofa. 'You're not going out looking like that.' She was brushing the jacket with aggression now.

'Looking like what?' he asked and continued to gaze.

'You've got yesterday's shirt on. No collar or tie, and is that a gravy stain?'

Looking down, he scratched a thin brown stain on his chest with his thumbnail.

'Nope.'

'For pity's sake, get some trousers on. They'll be here any minute. I've pressed them. They're on the chair.'

He compared his pocket watch to the mantel clock for accuracy. Engraved inside the case were the words, *forty-five years of service*. Its gold plate felt smooth in his hand. *Was it worth a lifetime of work?*

'William, trousers!' Margaret stood licking her hand, patting down what little hair he had left, which had gone wayward.

'Stop fussing, I'm not meeting anyone special.'

'Not special, he says, it's the biggest thing to happen to our family in thirty years! They'll be here in a limousine. I'm not having the neighbours seeing you as your normal scruffy self.'

'*Limousine?* Shame they didn't send one thirty years ago.'

Margaret tutted. She remembered the bad times, too. 'That's as maybe, William. Now you behave. They're trying to do something nice for you.'

'I remember how nice they are.' Buttoning up his fly, he sat down to put on his polished boots. 'Queues of hungry men with hungry families. Remember that? Stood at factory gates hoping for work.' He stood abruptly. 'The clerk would look straight at you, then pick someone else.'

'Yes, I know.' Margaret stood behind him, holding the jacket by the lapels as he slipped it on. 'You were your own worst enemy, you and your principles. They saw you as an agitator. You relished the fight.'

Now looking his best, he turned towards her.

'Right was right. Who else was going to stand up for us? They blacklisted me so I couldn't work anywhere else.'

A car pulled up outside, its brakes squeaked. Margaret stood and wiped his face with her handkerchief. She stared into his eyes.

'All I remember is your principles never filled those kiddies' bellies. Anyhow, they're here now.'

There was a knock at the door. They both looked at each other. Margaret brushed her pinny down with both hands, then she opened it.

A young woman with long brown hair stood smiling on the doorstep. She was wearing a blue flowered minidress with white knee-length boots. Her discomfort mirrored William's.

'Hello,' she said with a little too much cheer. 'I'm Miss Hornsby, Welfare Officer. A busy shopping day awaits.' She turned and headed back towards the car.

William looked at Margaret. She nodded, and he set out towards the shiny limousine. As he placed his pipe in his mouth, he caught a look of disdain on the young woman's face.

'No smoking in the car, please.' She opened the door for him.

William sighed and tapped his pipe on the heel of his boot before climbing into the car.

'Now, Mr Haddock,' she began. 'I've been told to spare no expense. They've stressed to me that you are to receive the best that money can buy for your loyalty and service.'

William gazed ahead, his thoughts drifting back to Margaret facing a charity board, being lectured on managing her husband before getting approval for benefits.

'The works manager, Mr Stinton …' She continued to talk, but William did not hear her.

Stinton started as an apprentice. William not only tutored his trade but everything he needed to know about *us and them*. Stinton had chosen *them*, kept his nose clean and risen to the top. Well, it was much better paid.

He had refused to strike or stand on the picket line.

William's mind drifted further back as the car rolled ahead. Three forces comprised the picket lines: unions, police, and scab labour. Cuts and bruises had no discrimination; they affected all involved. The truncheons fell on skulls as hard as the hammers struck the steel. Both had a purpose. Both could draw blood.

At Coes, the sales assistant buzzed around, bringing suits, shirts, ties and even underpants. William looked into the full-length mirror behind the curtain.

How had it come to this, stood in a changing cubicle in just a shirt, pants and socks? What had happened to the proud young lion?

The curtain swished half open and a straight arm thrust in a multi-coloured shirt.

'Try this one, Sir. It's called *paisley*. It's modern and very with it.'

If that's with it, I'm glad I'm without it.

As he took the garment, William's thoughts turned to oily boiler suits, the heat of the furnace and the deafening noise. *No Paisley shirts there.*

'Is this what you do all day, take people shopping?' he shouted to the girl outside.

'No, I have to make sure we provide welfare for the staff and our pensioners.'

'So, I'm a pensioner now?' he chuckled. 'It beats being called an agitator.'

The clothes kept coming. William felt more and more uncomfortable. Once fully dressed, he pushed back the curtain.

'You look very debonaire. We'll take that. Pile it with the rest on the counter, please. Also, the brogue shoes in brown and black. I have a cheque to cover all the costs. Please forward the receipt, too. Ransome's head office. Shall we have tea?'

She was already heading for the door.

The Lyons Tea Rooms was smoky and full of chatter. The waitress in her black-and-white uniform rushed back and forth.

'Two cream teas, please, and sausage rolls.' Miss Hornsby placed a square beige leather handbag on the table. Discreetly, she pulled out a small hip flask. 'I've done my research. I understand you like a celebration?'

William smiled. As she poured a nip into the cup, going to stop, he tipped the flask a little longer.

'When did you start at Ransome's?' she asked. 'I think they're a good firm.'

'Are they?' William raised an eyebrow. '1923, just in time for the big strike. No unions or employee benefit like holidays.'

'I'm off to Spain next week for my holiday. I'm really excited. Where did you go?'

'Nowhere.' His thoughts turned to unpaid for shut down, no sickness pay, or paid overtime. *He'd had to fight for everything and here she was, off to Spain.*

As Area Secretary for The Amalgamated Union of Engineering Workers, his family knew the hardship of industrial action. He'd faced every management team since 1933, but none as formidable as Margaret. She could stop him with a smile. Or a left hook.

'Speaking honestly, my experience with them is great. It's why I can see the world and go to Spain,' Miss Hornsby continued happily.

'Do you understand the term slavery, Miss?'

'Of course, it's a vile thing – owning a person.'

'Yes, but to me, there are different types of ownership.

It's the difference between living to work or working to live.'

She stared at him blankly, and after a pause, she said, 'It's time to get you home.' She stood up and gestured to the car awaiting outside the window.

Homeward bound, William reflected on battles, comradeship, and laughter. Miss Hornsby was probably thinking of Spain, the sun and the sea, topped up with Sangria.

As they drew up outside Ransome Crescent, William eagerly climbed out.

'I've had a lovely day with you. It's been a pleasure meeting you,' said Miss Hornsby.

'Likewise,' William uttered. He turned to take his leave, only to be called back.

'Mr Haddock, wait – you've forgotten your parcels.'

'No, thank you,' William replied, not turning around.

'But – they're yours – your clothes?' Miss Hornsby shouted.

'They haven't given me anything before and I want nothing from them now.'

'Mr Haddock, they cost a fortune!' William could hear the disdain in the woman's voice. 'What am I supposed to do with them?'

'Anything you like. Poke um, sell um, I don't care. You tell them they can't buy William Haddock. Never could, never will. They know our history.'

The old blood boiled once more. The principles stood firm. William smiled to himself. Perhaps there's nothing quite like an old fool, but the small wins still brought satisfaction. He'd fought hard to work to live and not to live to work. Nothing could take that away.

Looking up, he saw Margaret standing on the doorstep, anger colouring her cheeks.

'For pity's sake, William! Get inside and stop making a show of yourself! Will you ever learn?'

Eye by Louise Carr

Eye is a beautiful, bustling little town close to the border with Norfolk, reached by the A140 from Ipswich or Norwich. Eye has been settled since pre-history and derives its name from the Old English for 'island.' It would have been surrounded by marshland and water for much of the year. It is full of stories, characters, and a sense of the long history of its settlement – the perfect place for a writer to draw inspiration.

The spark of an idea for my story came from a Heritage Open Day poster in the window of The Fabric Shop in Eye. It said, 'The earliest mention of trade in Eye was in 1673 when the women's employment … was the making of bone lace.' Pigot's Directory of 1839 records that 'some of the humbler class of industrious females employ themselves in lace making.' I was intrigued by these 'industrious females' and the industry they built, economically important for the town and a means of providing security for themselves and their families.

Bone lace is another name for pillow lace and was worked with bone or ivory bobbins on lace pillows. Women took up the craft as it was easy to learn and brought in more income than weaving, spinning, or sewing. Incidentally, the word *tawdry* comes from tawdry lace and is a corruption of Saint Audrey's lace; lace necklaces sold to pilgrims visiting shrines to Saint Audrey. They fell out of fashion in the late 1600s, leading tawdry to mean cheap, tacky, and vulgar.

Saint Audrey's Lace

Eye, Suffolk, 1673

Two knockings on Edith's door in one day. The first knocking come at lunch, when Edith has her crust on the table, drop of ale, fingers numb from a morning's making bone lace no one'll buy.

Least, she believes it was this lunch time. Truth be the devil's downfall, it's tricky to pin things one day or the other. Could have been yesterday, when the door swings open on that sloven Agatha Cratford with a face clung like hard soil.

'The lace dealer's gone, Edith Locke.'

'Grimstone.' The women won't use her true name, but it's what she is. Locke don't count no more. 'Edith Grimstone.'

'Says he's not coming back, *Locke*.'

'Not my doing, Cratford.'

Aggie's craning to get a glimpse inside and Edith shuffles into the space, door resting solid as a punch on her behind.

Nothing she hasn't heard before from Aggie or one of the other lace women. What's different is Aggie's come to her house, braved the mardling disapproval. Perhaps there's a chance for redemption. If she wants it.

Aggie pulls herself up to a barely significant height, sniffs like she's dislodging flies from her squat nose.

'It's all your *doing*,' she sneers. 'Dealer knows of your doings, and he don't want tainted lace.'

Tainted lace.

As if the linen threads plait a trail of blood around the lady's sleeve. Worsted wool carries the subtle scent of scandal. *Sniff on that handkerchief, my lord, and you'll know what it is to be beaten.*

'Not that you care, Locke,' Aggie persists.

Edith sighs, shifts herself to her better left side, the other crackling with a warning to close the door. *Get back inside Edith Locke and don't be thinking you can alter anyone's mind.* John were right, for all his fists. *Ain't nobody but me going to understand you, Edith. Nobody going to see the worth I see.*

'I care,' Edith says. Nothing truer than that. Lace has always been in her family and she's the best out of them all. 'We make the same profit as a man does through sweat and struggle, just sitting in the sunlight the length of the sweet day. We can't lose that. Without bone lace, what do we have?'

'There never was no *we*.'

'Now, hold you hard, Aggie. We keep together.'

'You've always thought you're better 'an us and the bone lace. You go too far. You messed things up for everyone; now he's not buying like the rest of 'em.'

'It's not me,' Edith murmurs. She feels the familiar creep of fear but she'll try, she'll not back down this time. 'It's the lace we're weaving; Saint Audrey's lace. Tat. No one's wearing it no more, that's why he's not buying. We're skilled, Aggs. We can make better. I'll speak to him, set him right –'

'I'm certain you will, Locke,' Aggie leers. 'Like you did your husband.'

'– we don't even need the dealer. We sell direct. I've been thinking –'

'What's the good of that? *Thinking*? With your head? Your *soul* is in peril, murderess! I know your husband were bad, but he were no worse than anything we've all got. I'll wager you took his thatcher's pole and jammed it in him just for spite.'

'Cratford,' Edith snaps, a rush of red over her eyes and the heady seethe of cow parsley in her throat, 'your toe's in peril over my cursed threshold.'

Aggie whips her foot out so quick she near falls backwards. Her black skirts crackle, stir up the dust and Edith steps back too, head pounding, the cool sanctuary of her room stroking the back of her neck.

But Aggie's not finished.

'Admit it! Throw out your lace pillow. Leave us be!' Aggie cries.

'I never killed him, snouty mawther,' Edith snarls, and finds herself staggering backwards, the door frame slipping free from her fingers. Something sharp in her chest, one thrust and Edith topples, knocking the pillow off its table. Another jab and Edith sees it's a bobbin, a long bulb-head bone one poked in her chest and though Edith is now skiddled on the flagstones with the scattered beads and the dirt, she chuckles.

Felled by bobbin.

The second knocking comes now.

Hollow thuds on the wood in the middle-night silence. Tentative, nothing like Aggie's. How long has she lain here? Edith pulls herself up. Bare feet meet flags as she leans against the open window.

Outside, the moon is cream as bobbin-bone. There's a close-woven silence draped over the lane. A figure is stepping back from the house. She's half expecting the dealer's leather-lean face to be beneath that cloak. It's late, but he did keep odd hours. She's expecting the sound of her own

51

voice with more plea that perhaps this time will make a difference.

But she makes no sound.

It's the laugh that stops her. Low and sure. A laugh she knows, that knows her. It's not the dealer, although the man spreads across his hand lace with the finest honeycomb eyelets she could ever dream of creating. He holds it up. The leafed tallies, the thin brides connecting them like spider's web, the thousand threads wound together into an unbreakable whole.

'John?' she tries.

Up until now she has never countenanced leaving. But as he drifts away up the shadowed lane, the band of lace unwinds behind him, trailing like a deliverance, spangling pure white in the dust, and she understands. She's done with Saint Aundrey's lace; she's been finished since John left. She's more than the pettiness and the bargaining. And she has missed him, for all his faults.

Her fingers search for the snick in the darkness to open the door and follow him. Yet the latch is not where it should be. Her toes tip against something bumpy, slumped. Now her eyes have a light seeping in and she sees there are no hinges on the door, no metal, there's no small hole for a finger to open it more easily. No scratched letters of his name, and the fear of him that has rested so heavily in her mind has gone too, and what a blessing that is.

No door at all.

Just her own body where it lies on the flags, eyes wide open, Aggie's bobbin rocking on the floor beside it. And a path of bone lace leading upward into the stars.

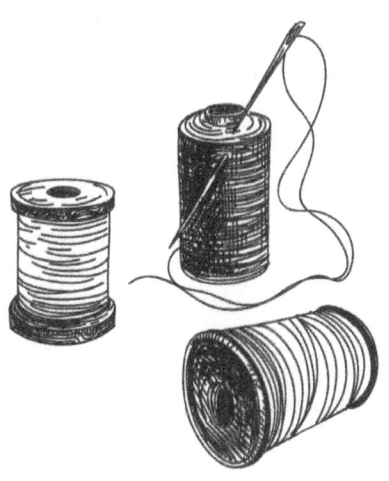

Minsmere by Charlotte Yule

On the coastline of East Suffolk, between Walberswick and Sizewell lies a stretch of rare lowland heath, home to critically endangered species and 37 breeding pairs of the red-listed Dartford Warbler. I have spent many years exploring this area with my dogs and children, mapping the heaths and woodlands that stretch between the A12 and the coast as we ventured further afield, leaving footpaths behind us in favour of the quieter less trafficked places where time seemed to fall away.

On one particular day, we had planned to walk on Westleton Common, which lies on the Southern edge of Westleton village. When we arrived, the carpark was full, with cars packed onto the verges forcing us further down Mill Road. Just before the crossroads, we stumbled upon a small area of woodland. Scrambling through dense bracken and spiny gorse, we followed a narrow twisting path which gave way abruptly into a wide expanse of heath. Narrow pathways fell away down steep banks of yellow gorse before climbing to a summit from where miles of heather drenched heathland stretched to the horizon, interspersed with patches of low-lying woodland. This landscape, with its sense of dislocation from the modern world, has been a source of inspiration and joy for many years. A place rarely frequented by other people, where nature quietly thrives and the walker, thinker or writer is free to immerse themselves in the truly unique landscape of this ancient heathland.

Leaving the A12 at Darsham, drive through the village towards Westleton. With the village green on your left, pass the duck pond, taking Mill Road straight ahead. Pass signs for Westleton Common and parking areas, heading towards Minsmere. Park on the verge on the right just before the open land gives way to woodland and take the narrow pathway into the trees. Turn left at the main footpath, towards Minsmere.

52°15'13.8"N 1°35'12.2"E

Between Westleton Common to the Northwest and RSPB Minsmere to the Southeast lies a stretch of undesignated common land consisting of lowland heath and mixed deciduous woodland. Unlike many of the surrounding landscapes, the terrain here is challenging with steep ascents and descents, narrow pathways maintained only by the native wildlife and thick drifts of thorny gorse.

The land here works for me.
heath and heather toil,
as rain patterns the sandy banks with pockmarked flurries
imprinting the landscape.
I breathe in the dampness,
mossy earth darkened by drifts of leaf litter,
sediments of ash, birch and berry-laden rowan,
and the hourglass falls away.

In this place,
where scree descends to woodland dell,
stretching to a horizon unpunctuated by chimney,
place becomes poetry,
weaving threads of narrative from the weft
of its rise and fall,
the undulation of summit to bowl,

heath to treescape,
heather and bracken beckoning towards gorse scented
pages,
where the thorny caress of my passage
marks fleshy parchment with nature's braille.
Lines of unbroken prose pour from this landscape,
footprintless, vast and mine to wander,
awash with birdsong, yet still,
a pause, from which inspiration ruptures.

The passage to the summit is narrow
and asks its toil of me,
sand sediments in furrowed pathways
where undulations of ink pool
parsing place into poeticism.
Hemmed between tamed wildness,
and cultivated wilderness,
the spectacle of nature-tourism conceals this place,
a reserve of temporal dissonance,
where, amongst the heather studded scree,
minds are free to wander,
and where my pen, ink flowing freely,
shapes the shaded slopes into significance,
mapping a terrain of discovery
onto the pages of my prose.

This land,
works for me.

Southwold by Molly-Kate Britton

Located in the centre of Southwold, just along the high street and not even ten minutes' walk from the coast, is Montague House. The former home of author George Orwell, though he was Eric Blair at the time, is steeped in history. However, I am more interested in the history that is not written down. Orwell's first wife, Eileen, died only a few years after they married, and subsequently fell through a memory hole in his legacy, despite her words appearing in his works. My story offers an insight into the marriage of Mr and Mrs Blair, before he was Mr Orwell, and how Eileen appears in his works.

Mrs Blair's Apple-Meringue Pie

In the small kitchen of Montague House, a scratched brass teapot sits on the gas stove. Eileen takes it from the heat with help from a thick cloth, and places it on the side, adding exactly six teaspoons of Indian loose-leaf tea. Behind the newly empty hob, a small brass kettle containing a quart of water is just beginning to steam.

While she waits for the kettle to boil, she adds flour, butter, and a pinch of salt to an earthenware mixing bowl. Eileen removes her wedding ring, the economical metal still far too new to bear a scratch, and puts her hands into the cubed butter and mountain of flour before rubbing it between her fingers until it looks like something reminiscent of breadcrumbs. A few drops of water are added, and she squeezes the lot into a ball, delivering a select few pinches to properly mix and shape it.

She does not do more than that. She hesitates to do as

much as she does. Pastry is delicate. One of the few things in life better left to its own devices, and after several failed attempts, she refuses to overwork another. She places the dough on a plate, also new, also unmarked, a wedding gift from her in-laws, and pulls down the stiff and cold handle of the icebox until it moves. She pulls the door open, placing the plate inside and closing it quickly so as not to let the cool air escape into the warm air of the summer afternoon.

She peels the apples next, four of them, taking her time to remove every piece of skin until not a spot of Bramley green remains, and dices them up.

Her husband's voice from the next room jolts her slightly. She almost cuts herself on the knife, adding to her impressive collection of nicks on her fingers, as he calls to her. 'How would you identify an anti-intellectual?'

'I find they identify themselves,' Eileen calls back. She is met with silence, and continues with her task, already accustomed to her husband's disappearing in thought, as if she were never there to begin with.

The apples go into a pan with two tablespoons of caster sugar, lemon juice, and another few drops of water, and Eileen presses the gas on and holds a match to the clean black enamel until it catches light, placing the pan over it.

When the familiar whistle pierces the kitchen, Eileen pours the freshly boiled water into the warm teapot, watching as the rich brown colour of the leaves begins to bleed before putting the lid on the pot. Her husband was far too particular about his tea for her to not know this, and each pot used so many tealeaves that it was a great shame to re-start. At times, she wondered if, given the opportunity, Eric would pull up a chair and observe her as she followed his instructions, ones he felt so passionately about as to write an essay on them, outlining the eleven steps to his preferred cup, which Eileen followed rigorously. She wondered, too, if her husband would ever follow his own instructions and deign to make her a cup, or if he was perfectly content to leave her to make his tea for him.

She tugs the icebox open again, removing the plate which is not nearly as cold as it needs to be, and a small pot of milk, carefully separated from the cream, before closing the door once more. The pastry is still pliable enough to roll and stretch until it lines a small round pan, and when it does, she places it in the oven.

She collects the teapot and a rounded breakfast mug and gives the teapot a shake to disperse the leaves. She hooks the mug on her little finger and pinches the milk pot between her thumb and empty ring finger before carefully carrying the lot to the study. It was a careful balance, one Eileen had picked up quickly since their wedding, only a few short weeks ago.

She wishes she were like the wives who came with these things built in, who knew, as if by magic, how to make a pie or a pot of tea or run a household the way they should, particularly with a husband like hers, who could disappear into his study for days at a time if permitted, and was even less help than she was at the best of times, but, as she begins to feel the small pot slipping from her tremulous grasp, only for her to catch it around the rim, she supposes those wives have help, and there is a certain feeling of accomplishment to doing them alone.

Eric sits at his desk. He does not acknowledge her arrival, and she does not expect him to, but when she sets the teapot next to him, he inhales and hums happily as the smell of rich tea permeates the air.

'I need a name,' he says as she turns to leave.

'A name?'

'Yes. Something to describe a place where one may erase

all evidence of something, as if it never existed to begin with.'

Eileen nods in understanding.

'What does it do to the people?'

'The people? They hardly notice. Most of them never knew it was there to begin with.'

'And how is it done?'

'Some form of disposal unit that destroys it completely. I haven't arranged the finer details yet.'

Eileen considers. 'It sounds like a gap of sorts. It was there, and then it wasn't. Like it died, and it left a hole in the memory.'

Eric nods slowly, considering, and Eileen takes this as dismissal. She turns back towards him to place a kiss on his cheek, which her husband does not react to, before returning to the kitchen.

The apples are the colour of caramel and when Eileen places a warm cube on her tongue, it has just enough of a bite to it to not completely dissolve in her mouth. She checks the pastry. It needs another few minutes, just slightly shy of golden brown, and so she busies herself by separating the eggs, dropping one, then two yolks into the apples and stirring. The pastry is ready now, and so she removes it from the oven and spoons the creamy apples into it.

The whites are put into a clean bowl, and mixed with a fork until her wrist aches, the way her mother taught her, and her mother's mother taught her. Eileen did not pride herself on her cooking, the way her mother had, but her mother was a housewife to a husband who could not afford a cook, and Eileen was set to be a working wife for much of the same reason, and so she was determined to build a reasonable repertoire of recipes. Snowy mountain peaks sit in the bowl, and Eileen sprinkles the remaining sugar over it, stirring again until it is thick and glossy.

She should hold it over her head, just to be sure it is sufficiently stiff, but eggs are far too much trouble to get out of hair, and so she turns the bowl upside down above the kitchen counter and waits.

One second.

While five seconds felt far too long, the recipe card said five seconds in her mother's neat cursive, and so five seconds it would be.

Two seconds.

It is stressful waiting for one's wrist and kitchen counter to be covered in egg whites. Eileen was quickly learning what it felt like to have the white sludge, sticky and scratchy with sugar crystals, flop from the bowl to all surfaces beneath it, and if her husband was any less attached to the recipe after tasting her mother's rendition, she would have abandoned it long ago. Her husband's memory hole, if that is what he was to call it, comes to her as if in a vision, and she imagines her eggs falling down into it and herself following behind.

Three seconds.

There were some things, Eileen knew, a wife had to do for her husband, and so far, she had faltered. Her work kept her from cleaning the house to the depth he would like, and their marriage was too new, and their work too unsettled, to plan for children, but cooking, while she had time in the week, was something she could manage. She does not think he meant a real hole, and yet it appears to her as something swirling and dark and empty yet full.

Four seconds.

If five seconds were, in fact, too long, her mother would have changed it, Eileen decides. The same way a boss would tell a secretary to not bother writing down a superfluous detail. With that in mind, she was determined to hold out all five of the ordered seconds. It was inexcusable, she felt, that she was able to take shorthand, a feat just shy of speaking another language entirely, but unable to follow a recipe written in plain English. Then again, her husband could do neither, far happier to write recipes and for her to take his thoughts down in the shorthand she had learned in school. If she were to fall into a memory hole, would Eric remember her?

Five seconds.

Satisfied, she twirls her fork around the edge of the bowl to loosen it, before turning it again, allowing the meringue to plop on top of the apples. She smears it with the same fork, spreading pure white egg and sugar over the golden pastry and apples.

When everything looks pretty, it is returned to the oven.

She has twenty minutes. Eric's typewriter dings loudly from the study.

Laundry needs doing, she remembers, and leaves the warmth of the kitchen for the cool hallway.

As she passes the study, her husband's voice carries into the hallway. 'Word for upset, ideally starting with d?'

'Distress,' she replies as she reaches the sitting room. 'Distraught, devastated, destroyed.' She runs out of words as she picks up a pair of pants and folds them quickly, placing them to one side, the start of a stack. It all felt very domestic, and Eileen was determined to prove herself as adaptable to the home as she was to her work, bouncing between household tasks the same way she bounced between various roles. She does not think of the memory hole, of the emptiness, of the fullness, of the reasons one may have to put something there. The typewriter dings again, and again, and once more only a few seconds later, her husband in the state he observes while writing, the one that keeps him fixated on the page, oblivious to the world.

Two bags of laundry and three piles – his, hers, and shared – later, the smell of sugar floods the house.

Eileen returns to the kitchen and takes the pie from the oven, placing it on the side to cool. In the study, her husband sips his tea and continues his work.

Ipswich Waterfront by Matthew Wiles

This story takes place at the abandoned R. & W. Paul Ltd building in Ipswich. The building sits at the edge of the waterfront and is only a moment's walk away from the Cineworld cinema and the entrance to the town centre. R. & W. Paul Ltd stands beside an old Burtons warehouse and has been walled off to prevent anyone from entering the building. It has since become something of a landmark for Ipswich, with a 29 by 27-metre art installation, designed by University of Suffolk graduate, Sammi Wong, recently being unveiled on the side of the building.

R. & W. Paul Ltd was originally a malting business before it was abandoned, turning grain into malt for beer and other products. I do not know why it was abandoned, but it used to be one of the major businesses in Ipswich, contributing to the waterfront port becoming a centre of shipping commerce and power early in its history. Since then, the building serves both as an echo of a past long since passed and a mirror for those waking up to the world and wondering what their future will be.

For some, that future is bright. For others, it is a quagmire of uncertainty, and the terror that comes with it.

Simpler Times

You look up at the building before you and sigh wistfully.

The building itself is dull and lifeless, coloured a muddy shade of beige and covered by black streaks of dirt. Blank windows stamped on the walls reflected the grey sky outside. Weeds grow along the bottom of the building like vines, or at least as far as you can see above the graffitied barriers that surround it. There is barely anything that marks the blank slabs of concrete as unique, save for a monochromatic sign with bright white capital letters amidst its black-painted background.

R. &. W. PAUL LTD

The name doesn't mean anything to you. You have no idea what used to happen behind those walls. You've heard something about it once being a malting business, but you have no idea what that means.

So, you start creating ideas of your own.

Perhaps it was once a brewery? Your mind formulates images of workers juicing and cutting up apples, mixing them into ciders as they ferment beers in giant vats. You picture them filling glasses and bottles and capping them with their own bare hands in lieu of modern machinery, pilling them into massive boxes and loading them into trucks and train carts (because there used to be a train running up and down Ipswich's waterfront; you remember seeing the traces of old rails along the path). You imagine those same workers drinking cider in pubs across Suffolk, cheering and howling at the moon like a pack of dogs.

Or maybe the building was used to make guns and bullets and other destructive material during the wars? You imagine men in uniforms (what kind of uniforms? You don't know. They visualise in your mind as a blur) slamming hammers down on blank sheets of burning metal. You see a thousand hands pushing and pressing plates of steel and iron into airplane wings and propellers, twisting wires and screws into shells to make explosive devices, filling hollow bullet casings with gunpowder and screwing knife-sharp tips onto them, and so on. You see the clean barrels of artillery guns being loaded onto flatbed trucks and train carts, containers filled with cases of arrow-tip-shaped bullets and egg-shaped bombs being shipped out to whatever front of whatever war was currently being waged.

You close your eyes and imagine the working people of the past and their busy lives. You've been having trouble finding a job for the last few years, so you can't help but consider just how much easier it was to find work back then. There were factories to build in, shops that didn't ask you for years of experience, and businesses that didn't turn you away at the first opportunity.

Simpler times, weren't they? Simpler times when things made sense.

Right?

You try to imagine what 'simpler times' means but can't think of an answer. You try to realise what those things that made sense back then really were but still you cannot find an answer. You try to think of what 'back then' even means, and still nothing.

The past remains a vague, nebulous concept. Nostalgia for a time that you've never lived in covers your vision in a rose-red hue. The building standing tall before you begins

to lose its non-existent shine, its mud and muck suddenly becoming more present in your mind's eye. It's almost romantic, in a way, thinking about the things (whatever they might be) that have come before you. But were they ever simpler? Were they easier?

You stare at the building with its dull windows and duller walls and its ancient neglect from years of disuse and can't find an answer.

You think of your struggles, your current trials and tribulations. You've been struggling to find a job – any kind of employment – for what feels like eons. Everyone either turns you down or doesn't bother to send you any kind of reply. Time and time again you try, and time and time again you fail. Your family asks you about what you want to do in the future, what you want your life to be, and you must disappoint them each time with the nebulous answer that you don't know and you can never know. Your future is an elusive, unclear creature that threatens to snap at you when you try to visualise it in your mind.

You don't know what the world was like during the times around the two world wars. Not really. You only know of work and working people's lives through second-hand accounts made by haunted survivors and doe-eyed storytellers. You don't know what it was like to walk in the streets of cities a hundred years past, eat their food, work their jobs and fight in their battles.

You know what the history books say. You've had the simplified renditions of old wars and worlds fed to you in schools through films and documentaries and history books.

But those times were never simple, were they? They were just as messy and complicated as they are today, unfathomable tales of politics and events that you still can't understand.

The sky above you begins to darken. You've been standing in the same place for ages, staring silently at the grey-walled symbol of a past long gone. You don't even know what 'simple' means, in your case, save for slicing off pieces of a problem that you can't understand and leaving only the haggard skeleton behind.

So where does that leave you?

Where does that leave you, a lone figure staring up at a dead building with no way of truly understanding the world around you and the path you are destined to walk?

Why are you even trying to find a job? Are you doing it to provide for yourself in the future, or are you trying to find one out of a sense of obligation, or a desire to not be a disappointment in the eyes of your family?

Are you destined to work to live or live to work?

Even now, you still have no answer.

None at all.

You look up at the building before you and sigh mournfully, spinning on your heel and walking away from the concrete giant, its lifeless exterior staring down at you mockingly.

You walk without purpose, without an understanding of where you are going or what you are going to do when you get to a destination that you can't even begin to fathom.

You have no idea of what your work may be or what your future may hold ...

And that terrifies you.

Ipswich by Kizzy Barrow

For me, the landscape of my home county is inextricably linked with the idea of work and of *working the land*. Generations of East Anglians have worked their influence over Ipswich and its surrounding villages, and today it is complexly situated between rural and urban sensibilities, both geographically isolated from larger southern cities and yet now a university and commuter town, rapidly attracting Londoners and development.

To write the pastoral images of plough and field and harvest was a strong impulse when I considered work and the landscape I grew up in. I think that remembering the history of land is to honour it, and I feel strongly moved by the fields and pastures of East Anglia – but it is today's Ipswich that I wanted to write. I wanted to recognise the instability in the rural idyll, the absurdness of who – in our mind's eye – we imagine naturally having guardianship of land: the strong-backed and physically able, those with wealth and means.

If you visit the town square on market day, think of carts and livestock, of farmers travelling across the county to sell their historic wares, but also look around at the people that belong to this town today. As this collection is read, I hope it evokes not just an untouchable halcyon past, but ideas of the future of this landscape, this town and land, a future that includes and benefits us all.

Anthem for the Already Defeated

Sue doesn't know, but she suspects she comes from peasant stock. She thinks the doctor senses it.

Must be nice working outdoors, the doctor says brightly.

So long as the weather's good, Sue offers, and the doctor laughs too much at this.

Well, you *can* work, she reassures Sue. I know you've taken time off, but the fact that things aren't getting worse is a good sign.

Sue stretches one leg out between them, shifts her weight, and watches her toes struggle against the side of their too-narrow shoe.

Sometimes it's better, the doctor is saying. To stay on your feet.

Sue feels a ridge of muscle slide gracelessly over the cup of her pelvis. Her face must change, because –

Oh ouch, the doctor says. Yes, I know, back pain isn't a fun one. The lucky ones are back to normal after a few weeks.

Sue nods. And the thumb? she says.

Yes, the thumb. Now I'm worried about that. She turns to her screen. So we'll give the whole hand another three weeks, see how it goes, then we can talk about going forward.

The appointment is clearly over. All there is left is the pep talk, the hedged optimism. Sue doesn't need it. She holds out the other hand for the doctor to shake, but she avoids it politely, peeling off her gloves.

I'll see you in three weeks, Sue says, and fumbles for the door's handle.

Well, only if it doesn't improve, the doctor calls, as Sue starts down the stairs. She nods at the receptionist as she passes, who makes a face at her phone. Sue has worked in admin before – she knows that face – but now she is a gardener, responsible for the grounds and land of a semi-rural second home, just outside of Hadleigh.

She's not paid as much as she should be, or as much as she *would* be if she were a man with a team of NVQ'd strong sons, their name embroidered on their polo shirts and leased builders' vans. Helen calls her a Jill of all trades and makes it sound like filth, laughing as she pulls her out of her second-hand men's waxed overcoat and plucks the whispery dry haw-blossoms from Sue's hair at the end of a day. It's true, her hands have done many things.

Sue walks home through town. She wishes that she'd said to the doctor that not only can she not currently lift a spadeful of earth; the strength has gone so that she can't even hold a barre chord, can't knead bread or braid Helen's hair.

I can stand though, she says to herself, for ten hours if I need to. I can wipe my own arse. I'll press buttons on a till and give change. I can go to the shops for a few bits. I can do the peasant tasks. Surely my hands know more than those ancestral hands.

They've cleaned toilets, and tailored dresses. Once, they mended a windowpane, learning the glass's brittle flex and the slow hardening of the putty. Those hands play old melodies, songs that have calcified into the bone. They whet good knives.

It was the Spring floods that had done it. Sue had spent

weeks working on the lawns, the riverbanks and woods of the estate. There were dead trees to be dragged from the river, sodden ropes haltered around and then the chainsaw applied to them on the banks. Sue had declined the offer of a body or two being hired in to help. She knew what that meant: over-powered vehicles churning up the willow field, men with an inflated estimation of their own common sense giving out orders and side-mouthed jokes. And when they'd been hired in once, they'd be brought in again, for every tree that needed felling, every ground works and river clearing. There'd be no place for Sue then.

Ipswich is busy. The Romanian man with the accordion sits on his deck chair in the doorway of a closed down department store. He is playing something with an uneven time signature that unsettles the English ear. It's surprising to hear, snaking through the streets of this small East Anglian town.

Sue stops at the market. The stalls are pinstriped in a traditional navy and white, with astroturf underlaying the tiered displays of produce. The market looks like it belongs here, in the old town square, especially the veg stall, which has *Quality Local Produce* printed above it. This same stall appears at just about every market in the county, but it's priced right, it's not pretending to be in London.

The fat man at the fish stall catches her eye.

Haddock, he intones. *Skate. Fresh fish.*

She smiles vaguely in his direction. He has huge red hands, swollen and oversized like gloves, with short, thick, purplish nails. The man's apron is a very severe white, but smeared around his jutting stomach is the occasional slash of brown and pink. She thinks that at the end of the day, the man must soak it in the sink with a solution of bleach and water. She doubts the thing gets thrown in with the rest of the wash.

The fishmonger moves his bare hands against the crystal banks of ice and rearranges the silvery fish, the tableaux of watery eyes and needling cold drips. Her back is killing. It spasms irregularly as she walks, driving bursts of pain into her right buttock according to some ineffable rhythm. Her hand doesn't hurt, but the strength is gone in the thumb, meaning her bag must be carried on the side of her body that doesn't want to bear weight. She pauses, aware of the knitting of her eyebrows, and a sour twisting in her mouth. She allows her face to relax.

She moves on to the veg bowls, running a finger along the cool gloss of an aubergine. She pushes her thumb into an avocado. She tucks two with give in them under her arm and picks up a melon, but realises too late that she can't hold it with just the one hand. She briskly releases her hold on the bag and hugs the melon to her chest, cradling it like a child. The avocados begin slipping into her armpit, precariously clamped between arm and body. Sue tries to catch the bag between her knees, but it flops feebly to the floor. She looks around.

The aproned staff are busy, restocking crates of leathery looking peppers. Nearby a woman is weighing out her apples, dropping them carefully into a candy-striped bag.

Do you mind giving me a hand? Sue calls over.

I don't work here, she replies, looking at her oddly.

Sue speaks more softly.

I can't bend down, she admits to the woman, who looks at her, assessing.

Sue had dressed smart for the doctor's. Those too-narrow brogues and dark-green linen slacks with a permanently ironed-in crease. A proper handbag, not the usual grubby tote – and she'd not yet readjusted her voice. It was a frame of mind, her mother had always said. A way of projecting certainty like a truth, a confidence trick.

Sorry love, she says to the woman. It's just that I've done my back in.

The apple woman looks relieved.

Oh right, she says. Okay.

She sets down her apples, gathers up Sue's bag and holds out the handles for her to take. Sue offers her avocado-less arm and the woman slips the handles over it, around her wrist.

Thanks, Sue says.

As she rounds the end of her street, the low sun strikes her full in the face.

The ancestral memory in the fine white bones of your hands, Sue thinks, in those worn tendons and slow, clever movements.

Your peasant hands will still work. They will hold pastel and pencil and paintbrush and capture the dark gully of Helen's clavicle and the proud dip of her throat in the sun that summits the high-rise and spills over into the spare room.

Inside, Helen cuts the melon for Sue, fanning it architecturally across a plate. Sue smiles and eats it, curved yellow slice after slice. The juice runs down her forearms like legs of wine in the bell of a glass and the droplets catch the last of the light, like Man Ray's tears, like fish scales, like precious gems adorning her fingers.

Martlesham by Sarah Waterson

The story focuses on the land both within and around BT Adastral Park, which includes other technology companies, too. Before the site was built in the late 1960s and 1970s, it was an airfield. Throughout the First World War, the land was an aircraft testing site, becoming the Royal Airforce Aeroplane Experimental Unit, playing a significant role in both World Wars, as well as being a defensive station. The RAF and United States Army Air Force both used Martlesham Heath during the Second World War. The whole area hums with history.

Wider exploration around Martlesham will reveal the beautiful Suffolk countryside, with the river Deben nearby. The most direct route to Martlesham is via the A14, over the Orwell Bridge. Then take the A12 North, at J58, heading towards Lowestoft. After around two miles, Adastral Park can be reached by taking a right at the second roundabout.

The Light from the Stars is Old

It is the 1980s and each day Christian runs before work. He runs on land that surrounds his place of work, the same place his dad took off from, when it was an airfield during the Second World War. As he runs, Christian thinks about those Douglas Dakota C47 aeroplanes, their snub noses fronting the bullet-shaped fuselage, with a powerful propeller on each side from which sleek and slender wings projected. As he runs, Christian feels his heart pumping rhythmically and strongly, his breath deep and even, his legs moving smoothly. Blood, breath, body functioning at optimum level. This was his bliss, his joy: mind and body working as one, running, moving through time and space, as did those Dakotas so many years ago.

As he runs, Christian thinks of the planes starting up, the sound of their propellers, the smell of fuel, the pilot, his dad and the other paratroopers huddled within the aircraft with their parashoot packs as the Dakota builds up speed, rolling down the runway. Christian builds up speed too, as he runs parallel to what he thinks was the runway, within the site on which he now works, his legs moving faster, his body working harder. He tries to sprint after completing a ten-mile run, but it is hurting now, as he hits his maximum speed, hindered by gravity and physical limitations, as he imagines the Dakota lifting off and heading into the huge Suffolk sky, and fading back into the past. Though he knows it is impossible, he feels a deep sense of loss, of not being able to keep up with his dad and the Dakota, of not being able penetrate the past and to be there with them all. Instead, he needs to be in his present now. Christian resets himself. Engages with the day.

He gets into work early, his morning run glowing from clear blue eyes, and a sharpness of movement. He hangs his jacket on the back of his chair and sits at an uncluttered and well-ordered desk. There is a hum of quiet authority about him, a self-containment; he is a man with a mission, a man with work to do, never wanting to waste the day. He prepares as an artist may prepare before brushstrokes are applied.

Christian is a young man, with short blond hair and his posture is straight and purposeful as he surveys the day ahead within his desk diary. As other colleagues arrive in the open-plan office, he greets them with a cheery hello and a smile, before turning his attention back to his desk. But he can never shake off the feeling of straddling both the past and the present and he does not want to. However, his present, his time in the 1980s, is not that of the mechanical, of oil and fuel, of metallic flying machines, but of information technology.

Christian sees his screen as his canvas, his keyboard and mouse his palette. His dextrous fingers draw meaning from keys to screen. As he works, his typed letters, numbers and symbols cascade meaning into a world very different from that of the 1940s. He knows it is not a corporeal world that he inhabits here on the screen, it cannot be smelled or tasted and does not require strenuous, physical work. This is why Christian runs. This work requires brain power, not brawn, but he needs the physical in order to work this way.

He creates the virtual from his corporality, an irony that is not lost on him. The language is code, programming, and he is as fluid in its reading and writing as he is when running. He has considered this, and has decided that his is a job that needs both the physicality and the virtual: a curious IT ying and yang.

Christian feels in his bones that there was a dire need of airborne innovation in the 1940s, and that heft of historical energy seeped into the land on which another, more modern need has generated a vast park of laboratories and buildings. It is the birthplace of much of the technology used today, in 2025: the internet, speech-technology, phones and computing. Virtual youngsters, just infants back in the 80s and 90s: my, how they have grown. All around him they were conceived, were birthed, and Christian helped to bring them up, watched them evolve and his curiosity recognised the promise in them. He did not fear technology, he embraced it. Just as the urgent need for war planes fuelled a desperate need to embrace invention within aviation during the Second World War.

Over the last two decades of the twentieth century and almost the first two decades of the twenty-first, Christian has worked hard, worked on inventing the future, worked as a part the vast Suffolk laboratory site that was full of promise and exciting potential: the weavers of the virtual warp and weft that eventually became our web, our internet, our virtual world. When he first started working at Martlesham, the site was known as BT Laboratories, but as time moved on, the laboratories become a park and the park's name comes from the elegant Latin word, *Adastra* meaning 'to the stars.'

Now, retired and in his late sixties, Christian looks back across the decades of his career at Martlesham Heath: what was once the future is now the past, just like those war planes. With the stars, he sees them now as they were, way back in the past and Christian sees himself now as he was, in his past, as a young and eager employee. He sees his dear Dad, too, as he was back in the 1940s, as a paratrooper, heading out into the unknown. The light from the stars worked its way to the world, as Christian, as his father, as those across the decades at Martlesham Heath worked also, to become the history whose light can only ever come from the past, always posthumous and never present, though always bright with inspiration.

Christian, as an older man, still runs, and though his running route is different now, he still imagines the hum of Douglas Dakota C47 aeroplanes up in the Suffolk skies above him. And sometimes, he thinks he sees them, too.

Buxhall by Becky Holifield

Buxhall is a small village, to the west of Stowmarket. It is home to an historic church but is characterised mostly by its vast array of fields. The field in this story can be found roughly a mile down the long and winding road from St Mary's Church. In the centre is a large tree, under which livestock shelter. Usually, this field houses flocks of sheep; however, in my childhood, I recall it being home to herds of cattle.

The maternal side of my family hails from Buxhall, having farmed the land there for a few generations. As a child, I spent hours stalking through wheat higher than my head or running down the road away from chickens. When given the theme of 'work' for this anthology, my mind was immediately cast to my grandfather who, at ninety-six years old, has only recently retired from farming and moved away from the village for the first time. This story is a piece of fiction, although it is based on a tale told by my late grandmother, who was often perturbed by my grandfather's lack of punctuality.

A Borrowed Hour

On this morning, the first Saturday in July 1955, William awoke early to the rays of sunlight streaming through a small gap in the curtains. He pulled them back, taking in the familiar view of the fields. He knew the outlay of his family's farm in Buxhall better than his own reflection. His gaze travelled across the first field and rested on the second. The cows were huddled beneath the shade of the sprawling oak tree, eagerly awaiting his arrival. He dressed quickly, throwing on the clothes he had laid out the night before, and made his way out of the house. William was always late, but never for his cows.

The hedgerows had grown long, mottled spots of sunlight falling through the leaves. A trio of hares hopped from the grass verge into the wheat, their ears barely visible above the stalks. At the crossroads, William turned right. He could see the oak tree just ahead. Now the herd spotted him, hooves kicking up dust from the dry ground as they plodded over, baying in delight. He took his time, walking at a slow pace as they accompanied him in parallel to the gate at the far end of the field.

Feeling satisfied, he took a rare moment to relax. It was early enough that the farmhands were yet to arrive, so he found himself alone. This didn't bother him. He was the kind of man who took comfort in solitude, preferring open fields to the busy roads of town and morning birdsong to the drone of small talk.

He removed his dark jacket, hanging it on the side of the barn before taking a seat on the ground. He settled slowly, then rolled up the sleeves of his shirt to expose his already-tanned forearms. For a moment, he closed his eyes, allowing the sunlight to warm his skin. He set his hands out behind him, taking in the feeling of rough grass against his calloused fingers. A sparrow hawk screeched above, and he raised a hand to his forehead, using it as a shield from the sun. Years of working outdoors had etched heavy lines into the corners of his eyes, deep cut from squinting through the brightness. From his pocket, he produced a beige sunhat, floppy from years of wear, and placed it carefully on his head.

From his position on the ground, he began to study his fields. Rain had not fallen in over a month, and the earth had splintered, causing tiny caverns to appear in the soil. He watched as a trail of ants weaved their way across the parched dirt, narrowly avoiding the gaps. The fields them-selves had turned dry and brittle. William knew his crops were ruined, but he did not want to let it bother him. He knew acts of nature lay outside of his control.

He let a few moments of stillness pass before checking his watch. Quarter of an hour had gone by and it was time to return to his duties. In the distance, church bells rang out, signalling the hour. He prised himself off the ground, brushing a few stray blades of grass from himself before dressing for his chores.

Usually, he wore old clothes, content to muddy them with dirt or animal feed. Today, he did not have that luxury, and he knew that soiling his clothes would cause him issues for the rest of the day, so he made sure to cover them carefully. He pulled off his dress shoes, replacing them with well-worn work boots. Atop his pressed black trousers, he pulled on overalls, hoping to protect himself from the dirt. The arms were tied loosely together, and he took some time to unfasten them before tugging the sleeves up over his clean white shirt. He fastened the buttons in a swift, agile motion, then picked up the brown feedbag from its position against the wall.

The herd was ready in wait, eyes large and bright with anticipation. Their faces rested on the fence. The calves, young and bowed legged, peeked through the lower rungs. William pushed through the gate authoritatively, allowing them to encircle him. Their red coats blended almost seamlessly into the arid ground, matted with patches of dried mud. He took a moment to brush the dust from their backs. Their tails swished, sending flies towards their eyes, ears perking as William tenderly swatted the pests away. Holding up the hessian sack, he poured cattle nuts from the bag, listening as they clanged into the tin trough. He watched as the cows approached, vying for position with hungry mouths, their long pink tongues scooping up their feed with ease.

He stood for a moment, content in the company of his cows. They bowed their heads to the ground, sighing deeply in search of more food. When they found none, their gaze returned to William. He let out a soft chuckle and raised his hands in surrender. He had nothing more to give.

They turned their attention back to the grass. A calf strode towards its mother, stooping below her to reach her udder. William took his leave. He strolled out of the field and the gate clunked heavily behind him. With the cattle fed, he could attend to his other duties.

Once finished, he shrugged off the overalls unceremoniously, happy to observe they had done their job. The work boots slid off his feet easily and he begrudged forcing on the hard leather shoes again. He washed his hands quickly, drying them on the inner layer of his overalls so as not to dirty them. His suit jacket, which still hung limply on the wall of the cowshed, was warm to the touch, heated from the sun. It seemed a pity to wear it on such a hot day, so he draped it over his shoulder instead, vowing to put it on once he was in sight of his destination.

As he walked, he rolled his shirt sleeves back down, securing them carefully with cufflinks he had kept safely in his suit pocket. The cows followed him as far as they could, watching as he continued straight ahead rather than taking the path home.

The road bent, shifting and curving ahead of him. A single car passed, beeping as he stepped onto the verge. Eventually, William arrived at the church and locked eyes with a tall and willowy man: his father-in-law, standing at the entrance, anxiously waiting.

William watched as the car containing his bride-to-be looped another impatient lap around the road. He smiled, then took one last look over the fields. The farmer's arrival to his wedding was untimely, but for that, he was unapologetic. William was always late, but never for his cows.

Felixstowe by Caroline Roberts

Felixstowe Ferry is a quiet fishing hamlet north of Old Felixstowe, at the mouth of the river Deben. A foot and cycle ferry takes visitors across to Bawdsey, and a thriving fish hut sells the day's catch. I've walked along the coast to the village many times with my family and enjoyed a cup of tea, or fish and chips outside one of the cafés there, wrapped in our coats and hats on a chilly day, making the most of the winter sunshine. Looking at the weather-boarded buildings, the Ferry Boat Inn, and the boatyard, you can imagine the families who have lived and worked there for generations. I'm not from a fishing family, but I always worked in my parents' shop on a Saturday as a teenager and was desperate to join my friends in going out shopping, to the beach or to the local cinema. It was interesting as a writer to explore my own feelings about early work experiences but in a completely different environment.

Felixstowe Ferry

Max closes his eyes, letting the bob and glug of the motorboat lull him as it heads out of the harbour towards the lobster grounds. He knows the route by heart. Feels every shift and sway as they pass the shingle spits on one side and Bawdsey on the other, out through the river entrance to the inshore sea where the baited pots wait.

It's June, but the early morning air is chill and creeps up the cuffs of his frayed woollen jumper. Shoving his hands inside his yellow dungarees, he sinks his chin into the bundle of his scarf and pretends he's still at home, stretched and warm, deep beneath his duvet.

Every Saturday, he is hauled out of bed to go fishing with his dad, or down to the boatyard if the weather is bad, to run repairs or tinker in one of the sheds.

He thinks of the very first time on the boat, remembers running down to the little jetty, his dad catching him up and wrestling him into a lifejacket, laughing at Max's excitement. He loves it really, just him and Dad out on the water, but sometimes …

'Look at that morning!' Dad shouts as they near the first pot.

Max doesn't reply but opens his eyes and squints at the marble-blue sky. A gull squawks and circles above him and he watches it turn and flap its way back towards the harbour.

Max's dad peers out from the tiny cabin of the boat.

'Alright, Max?'

Max pretends not to hear and looks off to Felixstowe. His dad doesn't get it. His friends will be hanging out in town, like most Saturdays. They'll be going for a burger at the Wimpy and then off to see a film at the Palace cinema, if there's anything good on. For once, he'd really like to go. Jem will be there.

We might be back in time today.

But Max knows deep down that it won't happen. His dad will be oblivious once they start working. By the time they've unloaded the catch and washed down the boat, it will be too late.

His sister, Ellen, has a job at a café in Ferry. She spends her Saturdays serving coffee, hot chocolate, and endless plates of steaming fish and chips to visitors who blow in with their children and dogs after a walk along the beach, or a trip on the water. Max has watched them, snapping their artistic photos of the boats and the yard, smiling at the quaint, weather-boarded hamlet of Felixstowe Ferry that hasn't changed in hundreds of years, as his mum endlessly reminds him. *Felixstowe Ferry, where your dad and grandad always spent their Saturdays fishing, working hard and then coming in to sell their catch at the shop and down in Lowestoft.*

Max knows this story well.

'Nearly there,' his dad shouts, slowing the motor and steadying the boat above the first marker in the line.

Max heaves himself up from his seat, flinching at the cold fingers of his thick blue rubber gloves. He'd love to be working in the warm, fuggy diner.

'Ready?'

Max moves into place and his dad works the winch handle, turning it hard until a rope draws up out of the sea. The first lobster pot appears. The heavy, dripping cage rushes with water as it sways and steadies. Guided by Max's dad, it lands safely on the side of the boat with a scraping clunk and is pushed along the deck. Max sets it on the bench and unclasps its metal door, reaches in and begins to pick out the catch, measuring and sorting as fast as he can.

The sun beams now and they warm as they work, deftly pulling lines and landing pot after pot. Max counts each crab and lobster into the trays and throws back to the sea anything not yet grown up enough to be taken ashore.

He watches them disappear from his view, far into the deep. Imagines them drifting and exploring in the vastness of the sea.

Max checks his watch, willing the job to be finished. He works even faster, almost taking the pots before he's given them, clinging to the miniscule hope that they might make it back in time.

'Last one!' his dad puffs through reddened cheeks and heaves up the final cage.

Max grasps the pot from his dad's hands, unclipping its door as he does so. A stray claw catches his wrist and he jerks it away. The ragged cuff of his jumper snags on the clasp and pulls the pot, lurching it back over to the side of the boat.

'No!' Max jumps forward. His hand rasps hard against the soaked knots on the cage, fingers clutching at its frame. He wants to drop it, to shake the pain out of his hand, but he clings on by a twisted finger, struggling for grip against the tangled seaweed.

His dad starts towards him, an elbow cuffing Max's cheek as he tries to take the weight of the pot and drag it back onto the ledge. Their boots slip together as they struggle, each attempting to move aside but with nowhere to go. The boat tips under their weight. A gush of freezing water rushes up Max's trousers, breaching the sides of his wellies.

'Mind!' Dad shouts. He keels back, his hand reaching for anything to steady him. Max dives forward, just catching the lobster pot before it falls into the sea.

'I've got it!' he shouts, but the weight of it throws him back. He thuds to the deck, cradling the pot in his arms. Rough tails and claws of mottled red and black catch on his arm, but he holds on, wincing as the crabs and lobsters scrabble for freedom. With one final effort, he lifts the cage to the safety of the bench and secures its door.

'They're fine,' he says, breathing hard, his face flush against the breeze. But his dad is looking at him differently.

'Dad, what is it?'

The faint tracks of weathered lines crease around his dad's eyes.

'Nothing, it's just …' But he doesn't finish.

Max pushes back his hair and glances at the shore. His dad crouches beside him.

'You wanted to go out with your friends today, didn't you?'

Max looks down. The water swashes around his feet.

'It's fine. Really. I know you need me.'

A soft sigh escapes from his dad's lips.

'How about you leave me to clean the boat today?'

'But the catch?'

'I'll manage.'

Max looks up. A grin of thanks escapes him. He realises he's looking differently at his dad, too.

'Come on.' Max's dad laughs and turns back to the winch. 'Let's get these pots rebaited and head back.'

Max nods and looks again towards the shore. He will be back in time today.

Student New Angle Prize 2025

The East Window by Ben Collins
(Winner, SNAP 2025)

The village of Offton lies scattered about a small valley some eight or nine miles northwest of Ipswich. If you want to find it, turn off the B1113 at Bramford and head towards the village of Somersham. Keep on through the village and out the other side. Continue to the Limeburners pub – you are now in Offton! Turn left after the pub and follow the twisting road that leads to Bildeston. After nearly a mile, on your left, you will see St. Mary's church with its well-kept churchyard open to the road.

I understand there is a reference to a church in Offton in the Domesday Book, so the church's origins stretch back at least 900 years. The church, as it presents now, however, owes much to the Reverend Elijah Thompson, Priest in Charge of Offton from 1858 to 1903.

Years ago, I asked the church warden of St. Mary's about the little girl in Victorian dress who features so prominently in the east window of the church. In my experience, it seemed unusual. He explained that she was the daughter of the Reverend Thompson. The Reverend Thompson seems to have been a remarkable man who now lies forgotten under a broken headstone in a corner of the churchyard near the compost heap (therein lies another story). The story of the window resonated with me, particularly as, at the time, my own daughter was of a similar age to the girl in the window.

The East Window

St. Mary's Church, Offton

On the bench that lines the tower wall beneath the bell ropes, the rector sits in his own stillness and waits. Somewhere in the rafters, a fly bounces crisply off the ancient timbers; the sound of its aimless progress filling the void. Higher still, up in the belfry, the jackdaws – those unruly, unbidden lodgers – briefly chatter and squabble. An outburst from some farmyard dogs dimly penetrates the thick whitewashed walls and then it is gone.

With his hands clasped gently in his lap, the rector contemplates the fly as it continues its journey to nowhere, oblivious to all distraction, deaf to the outside world. His own journey through the years has been no more predictable, but the troubles and travails he has encountered along the way have been impossible to ignore.

When he arrived in the obscure parish with his wife and child and succeeded to the living more than four decades ago, the Suffolk church had cried out to him, begged him to restore her to dignity. *Mary, Mother of God, dressed in her sorry robes.* Other worries, though, had dominated his thoughts until *that* Damascene moment when he had realised his mission. Since then, he had toiled tirelessly in her service. Now, enfolded in her humble glory, his heart sings and he is at peace. He knows that when his time comes. and he is laid to rest in the churchyard, something of himself will live on within these hallowed flint walls.

His gaze progresses up the nave – with its black and red tiles – to the chancel and thence to the reredos behind the altar. There, emblazoned in Gothic script, is the ineluctable reminder of his creed. Clasping the crucifix at his neck with one hand, he begins to whisper his daily devotion.

... I believe in the Holy Spirit,
the holy catholic Church,
the communion of saints,
the forgiveness of sins,
the resurrection of the body,
and the life everlasting.

Upon *Amen*, the east window ignites in the early morning sun, staining the white altar cloth with pools of colour. He lifts his gaze and allows himself, finally, to greet his infant daughter. Dressed in dazzling white, her golden hair glowing in the strengthening light, she stands, heedless of his presence, in an attitude of perpetual prayer at the feet of her Lord and Master.

He recalls fondly the bitter tears that had obscured his vision in the months of mourning. How they had burst into rainbows one day in this self-same spot, when he was transfixed in a sudden shaft of sunlight that punched through the clouds. Wondrous had been the vision bestowed upon him and, at his own expense, he had tasked a master craftsman to capture it in brilliant glass. Thus, sorrow had been transformed into joy.

Whilst his stone-carved epitaph may grow indistinct with moss and age, Helen will continue, he prays, to blaze in the Lord's service for so long as the church shall stand.

Home-cresting by Louise Carr
(Runner-up, SNAP 2025)

My story is set in the Suffolk and Essex Coast & Heaths National Landscape. To find it, the Suffolk Wildlife Trust directs us to Tangham Forest, IP12 3NF, laying to the east of Woodbridge and Sutton Hoo, and north of Rendlesham forest. The Sandlings Heaths were, until around 100 years ago, a vast swathe of heathland alongside the Suffolk coast, an open land of warblers, woodlarks, grazing sheep, and blooms of heather and gorse.

I wanted to write a love story in short form to both this largely disappeared landscape and to the two women who have inspired my novel, which is set in seventh-century East Anglia. I'm interested in place and atmosphere, connection to the wild, and the untold stories of marginal people, as well as in how language shapes our experiences and our retellings of history.

Home-cresting

Sand Heath, Rendlesham, 650AD

Sky still as bones. Storm is approaching the sand-ling. Bracken whorled like snake, tense in this purple haze-scape. The man has finally allowed Tate heather-rights, to repair the hole in her roof, and that should mean relief, but Enna has come too. Unexpected, after their words this morning. Eyes vivid-dark, auburn cloaks swaddling her tiny body despite the middle-summer stifling, she snatches at stems until Tate can bear her no longer.

'Pick heather, not gorse.'

'What's the difference?' Enna pouts.

'Colour. And gorse catches fire just breathing on it.'

'Yet I prefer gorse. Smell of warmed butter, and poison-yellow suits my hair.'

'Do you want to burn down my hearth?'

Enna clutches Tate's sleeve as a night-bird lets loose its thought-rattling chur.

'I *want* you to know,' she warns.

Scud of mutton feet over the hollow brown ground and Tate's head begins to ache. 'We must beat the rain, Enna. We've collected nothing.'

Enna ignores her, waving a pale arm across the heath, over colonies of sheep chewing the wheat-grey ground, the silvery, heaven-blue butterflies roosting on the tussocks. 'I want you to *know* ... how badly your home-cresting fares against mine.'

'Home-*cresting*?'

Whatever Tate expects to hear, it is not this.

'Home-coming to these goose-turd flatlands of the east. Vision it. When you're wrung out from journeying, into a ... *swatch* of yourself –'

So triumphant over 'swatch.' Tate laughs, regrets it.

'Yes.' She frowns. 'I too have many words, Tate. When you finally arrive, but you'll never feel such giddy relief on cresting the last hill, looking down on your valley, your treetop tufts, the glint on your water. You'll never see your life so hoarded.'

'I know what it's like to come home.'

'*You* never know when your journey ends. Could pass Rendlesham, obscured by trees. You lose. You're never satisfied. All because *you* are of the Angles, and I am Northumbria.'

'Why must one win, one be defeated?'

'We claim we know one another, Tate, but we're so different.'

Enna draws her hand away and Tate feels its absence as soft earth from a lifted fingertip. Pitch of thunder in the purpling gloom and as it subsides, such stillness. Enna is hushed to the depths, all hissing, spinning passion felled, so Tate can vision the glistening thought in Enna's head, balanced on the needle-sharp between submission and attack.

Tate sets her jaw tight; ready.

'Why?' Enna demands. 'Won't you fight for me?'

There it is.

Words, like swords, must be chosen wisely.

'Enna, think how impossible it would make us.'

'We are impossible already,' she spits.

But she is unspooling. She smiles. A lullula warbler bubbles the air with the freshness of water-song, soothing and sweet. Tate watches her lover stretch, peel white slivers of arms away from her sides and hold them over her head.

'Tate,' she says, reaching to the bone-still sky, the first petal of rain. 'Tate.'

Tate waits.

Waits.

'Tate.' Her voice, insubstantial as smoke. 'Do you love me?'

Death on the Darsham to Dunwich Road by Sheena McCallum (Shortlisted, SNAP 2025)

The story that follows is set in East Suffolk, on a very particular stretch of road that I've driven with my family many times on our way to the beautiful forest, heath, or beach at Dunwich. It was inspired by my daughter's enthusiasm, when she was little, for pretending to kill pheasants on this road. (She is now a passionate animal protector!)

The journey starts at The Two Magpies bakery and café on the A12 at Darsham (highly recommended for delicious baked goods). From here, follow Hinton Lane towards Dunwich. It's a narrow, single-track winding lane that takes you first past arable fields, with hedgerows, large hedgerow trees and an abundance of pheasants. An attractive looking campsite is located halfway along (beware of oncoming campers and caravans). After a while, the vegetation reduces and the fields become sandier. This is where the fields of pigs begin, complete with impossibly cute piglets at the right time of year.

After the pigs, cross the B1125 Dunwich Road and you begin to enter the forest. Dunwich Forest covers 9 square kilometres with broad-leaved and coniferous trees and offers many trails and footpaths. If you continue on to Dunwich, you can explore this attractive village and beach. It was once the capital of the Kingdom of the East Angles, but the majority of churches, houses and buildings that made up this ancient capital have long been lost to the North Sea.

Death on the Darsham to Dunwich Road

Clutching her half-eaten doughnut in one hand, and Rabbit in the other, Issy tried again. 'Daddy, this is where you put my window down.'

The car window hummed its way down, just in time, and Issy clambered onto her knees, thrusting her face towards the fresh air. The wind whipped her long brown hair around her head, sticking odd strands to the jammy residues around her mouth. She wiped her lips furiously with her coat sleeve and pushed her head further out of the window, trying to set her hair free before raising her arms into position and cocking her head to one side.

The car bumped its way down the narrow country road. Issy wondered why Daddy drove through the potholes rather than around them. She didn't like the way they made her bones shake. Rabbit hated it too. They were coming up to her favourite bit though and she had her eyes peeled and trigger finger ready.

'Bang! Bang!' she shouted triumphantly into sharp Autumn sunshine, spotting the cluster of pheasants strutting and bustling under the giant oak trees by the field entrance.

'I got them, Daddy!' she shouted back into the car.

'Well done, lovely,' he replied, focused on the football commentary.

The rushing wind stung her cheeks rhubarb pink but, undeterred, she searched for more. This was the best part of the road for pheasants, between the bakery and the fields of pigs, where Mummy used to stop the car to look for piglets.

'Look! Hundreds of pheasants. Bang! Bang! Bang!' she shouted into the wind. The birds' green heads bobbed as they scuttled away from the car and Issy's shouts. One launched into panicky flight, following the line of the road in front of the car, to Issy's delight.

'Yes!' she exclaimed, sliding her head back into the car and looking up to the rearview mirror for Daddy's approval.

She waited patiently for him to speak before prompting him. 'Daddy, did you see? That's my best ever!'

'What's that, Issy?' He glanced in the mirror.

'I got them all. Mummy would be proud.'

'That's great,' he replied, pulling quickly onto the verge for a campervan coming the other way and not slowing down.

Issy settled back into her seat, mission accomplished, and turned her attention to the opposite passenger window. The pig fields were coming up. She leaned over, as far as the booster seat and seatbelt allowed.

'Daddy, piglets!' she squealed.

'Ahh, cute,' he replied, as a farm truck raced towards him.

Issy realised Daddy wasn't stopping and pulled Rabbit tightly into her chest, burying her face in his bobbled head. She remained there until they parked in the forest carpark a few minutes later.

'Come on, Issy. Let's get out.'

'No! You didn't shoot pheasants or stop for the piglets.'

'Sorry, lovely. I didn't know that's what you did.'

Issy looked at his face in the mirror and thought he might be about to cry.

The Wildflowers of Suffolk by Angelina Klein
(Shortlisted, SNAP 2025)

I wrote *The Wildflowers of Suffolk* to capture the divine essence of East Anglia, and to express how I have connected with its countryside over the years. The charming towns and villages, Aldeburgh, Sudbourne, and Saxmundham have always enchanted me growing up and have inspired my writing as I have aged. It is in these golden fields and ancient coastlines that I have found the plotlines to feature in my novels, and I can connect with the landscape intrinsically as I take strolls down bronzing country lanes or sit on Aldeburgh beach with the wind and sand swirling through my hair.

Aldeburgh can be accessed via the A1094 off the A12, and Captain's Wood, Sudbourne, can be accessed via the B1084 turning onto Snape Road, and from Snape Road, a turning onto School Road where you'll find a small wooden gate enshrouded by shrubbery. These places, as well as Saxmundham, are great choices for a day out and are charming all year round, although I'd recommend visiting Captain's Wood between April and mid-May, as this is when the bluebells are most in bloom.

These locations have brought a great amount of serenity to me over the years with their copper and emerald landscapes, and their stunning views never fail to bring poetic words to my mind. If you're looking for a countryside retreat which isn't too busy and in driving/walking distance from the sea, I would deeply recommend these towns and villages, all located in the East Suffolk District.

The Wildflowers of Suffolk

The landscape is different in Suffolk. There's something about the golden fields that make it distinctive and unlike any other countryside. Perhaps it's the wild springs of gorse that cloud its every corner. Bold, yellow-faced shrubs that last most of the year and brighten the forests of Tunstall and Saxmundham. Yes, the flowers possess some divine quality here, one which separates them from those deep-blue cornflowers of the Cotswolds. Awakened by the early morning sun, hydrangeas and petunias exhale an aroma like no other – rich, pungent, delectable – and I know that I am home.

Then there's the hollyhocks that climb around the cottages of Aldeburgh. They're in abundance here for the later part of the year, and their magenta and vanilla heads always make me smile as I stroll down Church Walk to St Peter and St Paul's. I've spent many an hour writing about their beauty, doing everything I can to capture it within my characters' minds, and they know that, for as I pass, they release the most gorgeous fragrance.

Then I arrive at Aldeburgh Parish, and thousands of dandelions tangle throughout the grass. When I was younger, I used to wonder how they lasted so long into October. It seemed to me that death had not reached the cemetery, for everywhere I looked, there was colour, and an elm tree shaded an oak bench where I would sometimes sit and think. Hollyhocks scrambled over the crumbling stone walls, too, and chimneys beyond gave way to drapes of wisteria and ivy that gazed out at the North Sea. Yes. The warmer seasons lasted longer here, and spring would always come early as daffodils burrowed their way through the earth at the church's gates.

The most beautiful place to visit in spring, though, isn't Aldeburgh. It's Captain's Wood. Growing up, I'd always been fascinated by its great oak and chestnut trees, and how thick green foliage would envelope the sky so that sunlight could only gently touch the ground. The bluebells there aren't like the bluebells anywhere else. Buried within the depths of Sudbourne, they grow with wild abandon and scatter themselves furiously into a violet carpet that blankets the dirt. Something about them not being famous or well-known makes them beautiful, and it feels like my own little corner of the world as the stoic trees utter their ancient whispers around me.

But the bluebells of Sudbourne do not belong to me – nor does any other part of Suffolk. The foaming sunflower fields. The great elm and birch trees that aisle the dual carriageways. The rivers flowing between deep lavender pastures. Gleaming in the setting sun, the landscape exists to be admired by the dogwalker taking a woodland stroll or the driver glancing over the Orwell Bridge on their commute home. It isn't there for anyone to own – and I think that's what makes it so unique. Gorgeously raucous, it will grow with us and beyond us in its own enchanted way.

Threads of East Anglia by Mika
(Shortlisted, SNAP 2025)

I wrote this piece to hold together the fragments of East Anglia that have stayed with me – places I've walked through, moments I've witnessed, people I've seen and remembered.

There's something about this region that feels stitched together by time. You can see the past and the present brushing shoulders: a farmer with a tablet in one hand and soil in the other, or a ceilidh band playing to a village hall full of every generation.

The story moves between Bury St. Edmunds, Southwold, Norwich, the Fens, Lavenham – places I've been through and thought about often. They're full of contrast: sea and soil, silence and song, tradition and change. I didn't want to focus on just one location, but instead let the story move like a thread pulling through the fabric of East Anglia – connecting lives, landscapes, and memory.

This region holds a particular kind of rhythm. You can hear it in church bells and market stalls, in footsteps on old cobbles and laughter on the coast. I wanted to write something that felt like a quiet celebration of that. The everyday. The ordinary made meaningful by time and community.

Threads of East Anglia

The bells of St. Edmund's rang out across the market square, their chimes weaving through the crisp morning air. The old streets of Bury St. Edmunds bustled with life – young parents pushing prams, elders resting on wooden benches, their hands curled around cups of tea from the corner café. The scent of fresh bread from the baker's stall mingled with the tang of sea air, carried inland from the Suffolk coast.

At the harbour in Southwold, fishermen pulled in their nets, their voices rising in laughter, as a group of children in brightly-coloured wellies searched for crabs in the rock pools. The lighthouse stood proud, a sentinel watching over generations who had made their living from the sea. Not far away, a couple walked arm in arm, eating chips from paper cones, the salt and vinegar stinging their fingers. They laughed, whispering childhood stories of when they'd done the same with their grandparents.

In Norwich, the lanes hummed with the chatter of students and street performers, their music mixing with the clatter of coffee cups in hidden courtyards. A woman with a Norfolk broads accent sold homemade jams and honey at the farmer's market, her hands moving with practised ease as she arranged her wares beside a younger girl – her daughter – who scrolled through her phone between customers.

Beyond the city, the wide-open fields of the Fens

stretched towards the horizon, where tractors rumbled through rich, black soil. An old farmer, his face creased like the land he worked, leaned on a gate, watching his grandson – fresh from university – examine the earth with the same reverence, but armed with data on a tablet. The old ways and the new, side by side, the cycle unbroken.

As evening fell, lights flickered in the thatched cottages of Lavenham, their crooked beams leaning into the stories they had held for centuries. In a village hall, a ceilidh band struck up a tune, and young and old alike took hands, their feet moving in time with the music, just as they always had. At the same time, in a pub by the River Orwell, a group of friends raised their glasses to the future, while an elderly man nodded along, a twinkle in his eye, knowing that some things – like the warmth of a Suffolk welcome – never truly change.

East Anglia, old and new, steady and shifting, tied together by the land, the sea, and the people who call it home.

Back to the Sea by Amy Rehbein
(Longlisted, SNAP 2025)

Growing up in the seaside town of Harwich, Essex, I've always had an affinity for the sea and fondly remember the number of exciting times I had down the beach. Even when I moved away to London for university and then to Ipswich, the sea always seemed to be a part of me.

Watching my nieces and nephews play on Felixstowe beach one day brought back all those childhood and teenage memories of growing up by the sea, and this is where my inspiration for 'Back to the Sea' came from. The piece itself takes place in both Harwich and Felixstowe, two places that look so close to each other but are yet so far apart. Diving back into these memories took me on an emotional journey of reminiscence and love for the East Anglian coastline. This emotional journey kickstarted mine and my husband's decision to move to Felixstowe, which we did earlier this year. We haven't looked back.

To get to Harwich, take the A12 at Ipswich and join the A120 at Colchester. Once you arrive, follow the signs to the seafront, and take in the gorgeous seascape. Felixstowe is accessible from Harwich via the Foot Ferry, but if that doesn't tickle your fancy, Felixstowe lies at the end of the A14. Make sure you visit the seafront, get some chips and doughnuts, and perhaps read 'Back to the Sea.'

Back to the Sea

Seeing her play on the golden sand, building sandcastles, picking up stones, running with glee to throw them into the murky depths, never to be seen again. Watching her take off her small trainers to dip her feet into a fraction of the North Sea and hearing screeches as she feels the iciness of the water. She should be scared, but she laughs hysterically as the gulls flurry around her in hordes. All of this takes me back. To a time when life was simpler, when life wasn't one big mess. Just me, being alive for the moment. This takes me back to the sea.

The salty sea air in my lungs as I ran into the water at full pelt. Gasping for breath when I realised how cold the water was. My mum's voice as she shouted at me not to swim too far, unless I wanted to be swept away and end up in the Netherlands. Sea salt on my lips as I dived under the water, my eyes stinging as I emerged for air.

Summer days spent with friends, picking out our favourite spot under the abandoned lighthouse, securely bolted, blocking our taste for exploring. Burying each other under the sand until only our heads were showing. The laughter as we tried to emerge from our sandy graves, the sand getting everywhere. Going to the only tap for miles to try and wash it off but never succeeding.

The unofficial school leavers party, 2009. Tents scattered

along the sand, the smell of cigarette smoke in the air. Cans of beer hissing as they are popped open, the malty smell almost overpowering. Teenagers staggering, clutching bottles of blue WKD, hugging everyone in their path. Drunken debauchery all around.

Walking along the seafront, my hand in his. The soft whooshing sound of the waves calming my nerves as we sit on the sea wall. The butterflies emerging in my stomach as he looks into my eyes and kisses me softly under the growing sunset.

Going back to visit in my final year of university. Photographing the sunset-ridden seascape, oranges and reds merging perfectly. My heart pounding, as I stand and admire the beauty of it all. The love and admiration for the Suffolk coast coursing through me, a tear falling down my cheek.

'Why do you love the seaside so much?' she asks, clutching my hand, gritty sand rubbing off on it. I could give her an abundance of reasons, but I just say, 'It's a part of me and always will be.'

She smiles, dragging me off towards the shimmery glow of the beach. That, more than anything, takes me back to the sea.

The Rising Tide by Ashton Turner
(Longlisted, SNAP 2025)

'The Rising Tide' is set along the beautiful Suffolk coastline and was inspired by the powerful connection between people and the sea. I have always found coastal places some of the most unique and fascinating locations, and for this short story, I imagined a small seaside town, based on places like Southwold, Dunwich, and Aldeburgh. These areas are known for their lighthouses, quiet beaches and deep links to fishing and maritime history. Since moving to Suffolk over ten years ago, I've enjoyed regularly visiting these villages, whether that be for winter walks or to take in the cooling sea air on warm summer days.

The story explores how the sea can hold memories and emotions, especially for those who live near it. The lighthouse in 'The Rising Tide' stands not just as a physical landmark but as a symbol of memory, resilience, and loss. The inclusion of the physical structure was partly inspired by a recent read, *The Murder Game* by Tom Hindle, where the lighthouse served as a symbol of remembrance and heartbreak to the characters in the book.

Suffolk's coast, with its changing skies, shifting tides and peaceful but wild atmosphere, felt like the right setting for Arthur's story. This landscape helped to shape the mood and meaning behind this short piece.

The Rising Tide

A man perched on the water's edge, perplexed by the vast emptiness before him, possessed by his past. They say there's no greater connection than that between a fisherman and the sea. Yet, for Arthur, that connection has rumbled and tumbled inside of him for many years.

The low murmur of the tide mingled with the whisper of the wind. The evening summer sky was like a canvas of darkening hues, hinting at the return of Arthur's old foe: cumulonimbus.

The steady shaking of Arthur's veteran vessel shafted his steaming cup of Bovril from its perch. Fellow old fishing smacks stopped bobbing on the waves and began bashing. Metallic bells rang raggedly in the gusts, which grew longer, louder, and more relentless with each passing moment. The band had returned with a vengeance of backup singers, shifting the colours of the sky.

The tide appeared drawn to the horizon, waves rolling in and out, its rhythm as sporadic as Arthur's heartbeat. It was happening again. The movement, the sounds, the lights, the smell and the cold, damp air scratching against his unshaven face.

Arthur squinted and searched for the lighthouse through the heavy, swirling air surrounding him. It was a beacon, a watchtower. An eye in the wind and the waves and in Arthur's washed-up mind.

The lighthouse stood as a great guardian of the land and a friend to those navigating the notoriously nefarious waves. It stood resolute, protecting not only the ships ashore but the jumble of brickwork which the townsfolk called home. The lighthouse honed a single ghostly white colour where its once red bands had now faded. The missing crimson is not forgotten; it lingers in the whispers of the waves, a silent tribute to the blood of those lost to the sea.

My blood, thought Arthur. *My blood*.

The sudden flash of light in the heart of the North Sea snapped Arthur back to reality. He couldn't be paralysed in the midst of the battle. Not again.

He moved with practised urgency, securing ropes, checking knots, and lashing down anything that might once again be so cruelly swept away forever. His hands, a direct contrast to his frantic mind, tightened the sail with such precision that instinct had engulfed his work.

He had done all he could to brace for the fury that loomed on the horizon. The air was thick with salt and tension, the sky darkened further as if the ocean itself were holding its breath.

'If you are alone a lot, you learn to rely on yourself.' Arthur had come to understand this truth more than most, his parents' horrific kidnapping by the merciless sea forever etched in his mind, shaping the way he faced the world – solitary, self-reliant, and unyielding in the face of the vast, unforgiving waters.

It was happening again. The rising tide.

The Marsh Road by Lauren Searle
(Longlisted, SNAP 2025)

I grew up in east Suffolk, spending most of my time outdoors, particularly on horseback. Riding through fields, lanes and bridleways gave me a strong connection to the landscape, its quiet rhythms and deep sense of history. Suffolk has always been my home and I've long been interested in how stories, especially local folklore, become part of how we understand and experience a place.

The Marsh Road is a fictional story set near Orford, an area I have always found both beautiful and atmospheric. It follows Alice as she returns to her grandmother's cottage and finds herself caught between memory and something more unsettling. The story draws on the legend of the Black Shuck, a ghostly dog said to haunt the East Anglian coast and explores how folklore can influence the way we view even the most familiar places.

Although the story is imagined, the setting is rooted in real Suffolk landscapes. The coastline, marshes and quiet rural roads all hold a certain tension and I wanted to reflect that in the tone of the piece. The story is about returning to somewhere you thought you understood and discovering that it still holds its own secrets.

The Marsh Road

The road to Orford was empty but for a fox that darted across the broken tarmac, vanishing into the whispering. Alice gripped the steering wheel, the headlights catching the silver gleam of frost on the hedgerows. East Anglia was a land of ghosts: marshes that swallowed ships, abbeys crumbling into the sea, legends that clung to the mist like breath on glass.

She hadn't been back in years.

Her grandmother's cottage sat at the edge of the Alde, the river curling like an old scar towards the shingle spit. The house was dark except for a single light in the upstairs window. Alice frowned. She hadn't told anyone she was coming.

Inside, the air smelled of damp wood and rosemary. The walls bore the same uneven plaster, the fireplace still stacked with logs. Everything was as it had been apart from the book on the table.

She picked it up.

The Black Shuck.

A childhood fear stirred in her chest. The legend of the Black Shuck was an old one, whispered by schoolchildren and pub storytellers alike; a ghostly hound with burning red eyes, an omen of death. She had heard the stories in this very house, huddled under a woollen blanket, her grandmother's voice lilting with the wind outside.

A sound creaked from the hallway.

Alice spun around, her breath sharp in the cold. The stairs groaned as she climbed them, the air thick with the scent of salt and bracken. The door to her grandmother's bedroom stood ajar. She pushed it open.

A figure sat by the window, silhouetted against the moonlit marsh.

Alice gasped.

The woman turned. It was her grandmother – but younger, impossibly so. Her hair was black, her eyes dark pools of knowing.

'You shouldn't have come back,' the woman said. Her voice was distant, as if carried from across the estuary.

Alice tried to speak, but her throat was dry.

'The Shuck follows blood,' the woman continued, 'and you are the last.'

A chill ran through Alice's bones.

She took a step back. The floor groaned.

From the marsh, a howl rose, a sound that sliced through the stillness, ancient and hungry. The woman turned back to the window. 'Now it's too late.'

Alice ran. She fled down the stairs, out into the night, her breath steaming in the frozen air. The road stretched ahead, endless and dark.

Then, movement.

A shape loomed from the mist.

Two red eyes burned in the darkness.

The Black Shuck.

Alice's scream never left her lips.

By morning, the marshes were quiet once more. The cottage stood as it always had, watching the tide creep in.

And on the road to Orford, the frost melted slowly,

leaving only a single set of footprints leading towards the river, before vanishing altogether.

Vikings in the Second Meadow by Harry Searle
(Longlisted, SNAP 2025)

If you travel up the hill from Hadleigh (opposite the junction leading to Morrison's, QD, and the like) and follow the winding country roads, you'll shortly stumble upon the quiet village of Whatfield. Bearing left at the 'green grass triangle' where the village sign stands tall, and left again by the designated bottle banks, you'll find yourself upon Rectory Lane. Head past the school and village hall and continue along until you find a wooden gate exactly on the corner as the road curves to the right. This gate marks the beginning of the stretch of land known affectionately to Whatfield locals as the 'second meadow,' and through this gate, you can follow the well-walked fields towards Kersey, or Semer, or even back to Hadleigh.

A prominent memory of my time in Suffolk has been the simple act of walking across these very fields with my family and our dogs, and so the idea to set a poem within this tiny piece of Suffolk came to be. Weaving the county's Viking heritage (having studied history as an undergraduate, I had to) into a simple afternoon dog walk seemed fitting, as these raiders roamed the same lands *en masse* over a thousand years ago. Yet walk across these fields now and you'll find no trace of them ever being here, their time in history since come and gone, and that we, now, have taken their place as the wanderers across the ancient green of Suffolk.

Vikings in the Second Meadow

Down in the second meadow I saw them,
Vikings they seemed at a glance, on old Guthrum's land.
Booted and coated – royal attire with frayed hem,
My mother and father, holding gloved hand in gloved hand,
Wearing knitted crowns. It appeared they never said
To wander that way before, with two dogs running off ahead
And disappearing into the near clutch of green grove.
Fallen sticks were gathered, or iron weapons stored
For later purpose – noble squires in loyal chord,
Led on through thickets along the path inwove.

Down in the second meadow I saw them,
I thought my mother wielded a sword, my father too.
Each a gnarled and knotted blade, a tree-forged stem
Brandished to vanquish evil foe, to charge on through
Housecarl flanks; to throw for dogs to retrieve once seen.
But how they looked like warriors then, with dullen glean
Of sticks or swords as they both marched onward, abreast
Down through stony track, crackling gravel beneath
Their feet, winding on through mossy heath
And heading away past beet fields, on certain quest.

Down in the second meadow I saw them,
And I saw them with two muddy dogs, lately returned

From pillaging the unmapped fen in chief mayhem.
How they churned that thick mud when they ran, spurned
Wild amongst the wild; wide eyes and claggy paws.
While one laid on springy grass – rests – the other draws
Close and with swings of arms, those swords flew
Arcing against the sun. Twirling javelins, then chased
Soon after by the dogs fast in such perilous action, abased
If failed to catch the sticks of those that threw.

Down in the second meadow I saw them,
Amongst the ancient land, in hedged wilderness.
Warm-faced by blazing cold sky, removed woollen diadem,
Before going whence, they came with quiet acquiesce.
Up along well-footed paths those Vikings returned;
My mother and father. While the dogs yearned
To run, they stayed patient, collared to woven tether.
Sticks now left behind, with teeth marks impressed
On those swords scattered across the field of contest,
Soon overgrown with darnel, drake, heather.

Down in the second meadow I saw them,
And they had seemed like Vikings upon first look.
Not dressed in leather or gold imbued with radiant gem
Or precious stone, yet travelled people from another nook
Of the world, walking the same fields as done in prelude
By forebears, raiders, kings and those which ensued
In long years since. My mother and father, since home
Hang up uncrowned hats, store away boots and coats,
Return to their work in easy rhythm fashioned in rotes,
Presently content with settled wilds but will yet roam.

The River's Dew by Jade Darton
(Longlisted, SNAP 2025)

'The River's Dew' is a poetic short story set in Woodbridge, a picturesque location that has always been close to my heart. This quaint town has provided me with a soothing refuge during some of the more challenging periods in my life. I found solace in the early mornings by the river's edge, nestled conveniently behind the train station. I would often sit watching the small boats bobbing gently in the water, their reflections shimmering with the first rays of sunlight. The stillness of those mornings allowed me to gather my thoughts and ease my mind as the rest of the world slowly awakened around me.

Woodbridge, which is just a short train ride from Ipswich, lies between the villages of Westerfield and Melton. It's easily accessible via the East Suffolk Line or by car along the A14 and A12. The town is full of charm, home to independent shops, cosy cafés, and the historic Tide Mill Living Museum. On Market Hill, you'll find artisan bakeries and the old Shire Hall, while the riverside offers quiet walks past boatyards and salt marshes.

As an LGBTQ+ writer, I wanted to tell a story shaped not by conflict but by tenderness. 'The River's Dew' depicts a moment of intimacy and longing – two women sharing a sacred space by the river's edge, where their love exists free from societal scrutiny. In a world where queer stories are often shaped by struggle, I sought to write one shaped by stillness, connection, and the kind of love that feels natural and inevitable, like the river's flow.

The River's Dew

It smelled like dew. It always did.

Wet blades of grass caressed the skin of my palms and the back of my legs as I stretched them, throwing my head back and letting a soft sigh escape my lips. A small and thin cloud of mist flew out of my mouth and dissipated into the air so quickly that it might as well never have been there in the first place.

The town stirred with the quiet rhythms of the morning, the scent of damp earth drifting inland from the River Deben. The ancient tide mill kept a solemn silence while its weathered wooden structure told stories from centuries past. The echoes of gulls filled the air from the dockside quay where anchored boats swayed gently against their moorings.

I felt at peace there, beside the river. Far away, I could hear the mumble of speech from the markets. Nearer, a couple of tiny dunnocks sang, their chirping melodious. I imagined what it would feel like to raise a hand, extend a finger and have one of them land on it. With my eyes closed, I did just that.

Instead of a small bird, fingers entwined with mine. A soft laugh caressed my ears, and I considered it an apt companion to nature's symphony, if not its soloist finally making an appearance. I peeked through my eyelashes and found a cascade of reddish waves, falling on shoulders like the river ran through its course.

She picked a crocus flower from the ground, its stem tearing between her long, sun-kissed fingers. She was clad in dark clothing, a corset around her waist and a long skirt that billowed in the wind. Her black nails and dark eyeshadow reminded me of a desiccated heart safely kept inside a drawer. Whispers of horrific yet human words came to me, written by a gentle hand that caressed the heart and kept it with her, always.

She reached for me and softly tucked a strand of hair behind my ear. My heart, so alive, so joyful, accelerated. Upon the moving waters and the singing of the birds, I promised her my being. She was akin to the chill respite of the well-spring. My rose and my lily flower. And yet, more. No bud nor blooming petals could compare to the colour of her cheeks or the shadow nested below her shin, under which shade I wanted to lose myself.

Be my sky, she told me. Her voice fell like silver upon me. It was the song of the flowing river, coursing through my very soul. I told her *yes*. Just as the waters would always flow, and the dew would always shine brightly under her light.

Always.

Suffolk's Sanctuary by Angela Nowak
(Longlisted, SNAP 2025)

Suffolk really does grow on you. Before my family moved here, we'd only ever lived in cities, so swapping busy streets for open fields felt like a massive change – but it turned out to be one of the best decisions we've ever made. I wanted to share a bit of the atmosphere of the places that mean the most to me: Felixstowe and Flatford. There's just something about being near the water that brings a sense of calm. To get to Felixstowe or Flatford, you take the A14, a road we've travelled countless times, often with excited kids in the back and beach bags in the boot. We've made so many memories on long walks by the sea, and those moments are properly tucked away in my heart. When a refugee family moved in nearby, we got to know them, and spent hours wandering the fields together, talking about life, its twists and turns, and everything in between. It's those simple, honest moments that inspired the poem.

Suffolk's Sanctuary

No hills, just endless green fields.
Inviting walks to find peace to be seen.
Dew-kissed summer mornings, still and quiet,
This is Constable's haven – nowhere else one can find.

Flatford's charm, the river's flow
A boat drifts by, the current slow, but lovers don't mind.
The old bridge stands, the cottages neat,
Time halts here, in tranquil retreat.

Farmers toil, their work unseen,
Anchored deep in soil serene
Restless refugees' souls transported from Ukraine's hell
In Suffolk's calm, hospitable and kind.

Once in a while, walk by the shore,
Where Felixstowe's waves splash about
Whilst you can eat as much fish as your heart desires.

Silly gulls circling, disturbing the atmosphere,
Rightly so, proclaiming that a county like it, is not easy to
find.

Writer Biographies

Laura May is a writer from Essex. She is currently undertaking a PhD in Creative Writing at University of Suffolk, writing a collection of poetry that explores memory and time. Laura has had three collections of poetry published by Chipmunka, as well as a novella. Her work explores trauma, mental health and memory. Laura can be found on Instagram @lmaywriter

Noah Goldsworthy is a writer and artist with an interest in cultural and personal memory, intergenerational trauma, and mythologies of the ancient near east. Noah wrote his first short story, 'Frozen Thorns,' in the first anthology that University Campus Suffolk produced. 'Baby Shoes' was published in 2010. A mental Health Nurse by profession, Noah has always been inspired by the human experience, psychology, and human behaviour. He has a particular interest in the healing of trauma through cathartic fiction writing and reframing, and would like to develop this style of writing to use in his professional practice. Noah believes that in every human experience, art and healing can be found.

Amy Rehbein is a writer of young adult fiction with specialisms in magical realism and fairytale retellings. She is currently working on her first novel entitled *Second*

Wind and was longlisted for the Student New Angle Prize 2025. Amy is studying on the MA Creative and Critical Writing at the University of Suffolk as a part time student and is thoroughly enjoying it. She also believes that if you can dream it, you can do it, and this is a mantra she takes forward with all her creative work.

Sheena McCallum is a writer who grew up in various parts of rural Suffolk. The county holds many treasured memories from her younger years, although potato-picking is not one of them! She couldn't wait to leave Suffolk for the bright lights of university at eighteen, but eventually moved back to Suffolk many years later with her own family. Having fallen in love with poetry and always having wanted to write, she enrolled on the MA in Creative and Critical Writing at the University of Suffolk. Sheena loves writing both poetry and prose, particularly memoir, and has had poems published in Suffolk photographer Gill Moon's book 'Planet Suffolk' and the Suffolk Writers Group's anthology 'A Tapestry of Poetry'. Sheena has twice been shortlisted for the SNAP writing prize and has enjoyed contributing to both the Suffolk Haunts and Work anthologies.

Harry Searle is a writer currently living in Ipswich, Suffolk. He enjoys spinning poetic yarns within the genre of existentialism, and also appreciates the occasional application of said yarns to various historical subjects. Following the completion of a BA (Hons) History in 2023, Harry studied under the tutorship of the MA Creative and Critical Writing at the University of Suffolk, completing the course in 2025, with one of his poems selected for the longlist of the Student New Angle Prize in the same year. In his spare time, he (fittingly) likes to read a variety of books, as well as busy himself with various other pastimes, often creatively inclined.

Jessica Spence is currently taking her MA in Creative and Critical Writing at the University of Suffolk. Fascinated by the tools of writing and the concepts she can play with, she hopes to one day be an author that asks the questions in a narrative for all to enjoy.

Ben Collins, a frustrated eighteenth-century dilettante, did his best as a barrister for many years until he wandered into the teaching profession. After an uncomfortable stint fixed in one place, he now pops up in primary schools around Suffolk trying to inspire children to be themselves. In between times, when he's not sucking the end of his pen, he can often be found trying to derive meaning from jars of ink and pots of paint.

Roy Haddock is a writer who is passionate about keeping the Suffolk dialect alive. At sixty-one, he began studying for a master's degree in Creative and Critical Writing at the University of Suffolk. Roy has had short stories published together with poetry. Longlisted for the Student New Angle Prize in 2024, he has also had short plays performed by Eastern Angles. Roy came to writing late in life and still finds it hard to call himself a writer. However, his experiences on the MA course have shown him that opportunities must be seized and that everyone has at least one story to tell.

Louise Carr is a Suffolk-based writer with a deep interest in historical fiction and female-led narratives. She is obsessed with the history, archaeology and untold stories of the early Medieval era and is working on a series of novels set in seventh-century Northumbria and East Anglia. Louise is a two-times runner-up in the Student New Angles Prize and she is completing her MA in Creative and Critical Writing at the University of Suffolk.

Charlotte Yule is a writer and PhD student at the University of Suffolk. Her doctoral thesis looks at the significance of Cornish landscapes in the lives and writings of female authors from the modernist to contemporary period. Her paper, 'Authoring the Earth Goddess: Unplacatable Wilderness and Transgressive Female Power in Daphne du Maurier's *Jamaica Inn*' was published in *MEJO: The MELOW Journal of World Literature*, March 2025. Charlotte has worked in publishing and co-founded a charitable organisation aimed at promoting equitable educational and extra-curricular opportunities for young people in rural East Suffolk. Creatively, her work has been published in *Suffolk Reflections: An Anthology of Original Stories Inspired by the Waterways of East Anglia* (2023) and *Modern Nature Anthology: Responses to Derek Jarman's Modern Nature* (2022).

Molly-Kate Britton completed her BA and MA at the University of Suffolk, and is currently studying there for her PhD in Creative Writing. She is working on a novel about classical composer Alma Mahler-Gropius-Werfel. Her interests lie in historical fiction, as well as neo-gothic fiction, and the role of women within these genres. Her online series, *Lives of the Wives*, sheds light on the women behind great men throughout history. Molly's fiction and creative non-fiction has been published in several anthologies and journals.

Matthew Wiles is a writer living in Suffolk. He has written small fan works since 2017 and enjoys writing a mixture of science fiction and drama stories. Matthew is, at the time of writing, a student completing the MA Creative and Critical Writing at the University of Suffolk. He was the winner of a scriptwriting award promoted by the University of Suffolk and sponsored by the New Wolsey Theatre. In his spare time, he enjoys listening to music and going on long walks, and lives at home with his mother and stepfather and their dog, Murphy.

Kizzy Barrow is a queer, working-class writer and visual artist living in East Anglia. They grew up within the New Traveller community and their work focuses on experiences of class, land justice and environmental futurity. Kizzy completed the MA Creative and Critical Writing at the University of Suffolk and was a National Centre for Writing Escalator fellow in 2023/24. They are currently finishing a collection of contemporary short fiction and developing their first long-form work, an East Anglian folk-realism novel titled *Sundogs*. Kizzy also writes essays, creates zines and makes sculpture on the subjects of art history, folklore, traditional song, and resistance.

Sarah Waterson is a writer living in Suffolk. She has had short stories published in previous Talking Shop Press anthologies. Having completed the MA in Creative and Critical Writing at the University of Suffolk in 2024, Sarah will be embarking on a creative writing PhD, at the University of Suffolk, in 2025. She facilitates creative writing workshops and enjoys running and walking around the beautiful Suffolk countryside.

Becky Holifield was born in Suffolk. She returned to the county in 2020 after completing her BA in English and Theatre at the University of Roehampton, and spending time travelling. After an almost ten-year break from her studies, she is currently in her second year of the MA Creative and Critical Writing at the University of Suffolk. Becky has a passion for Young Adult novels and is currently working on a New Adult novel, centred around the theme of nostalgia. She enjoys walking, travelling, and can often be found listening to Taylor Swift.

Caroline Roberts is a writer and freelance theatre maker based in Manningtree. She is passionate about women's voices and creative writing. Caroline's special interest is the subject of motherhood in the works of Agatha Christie, which she is exploring through her PhD at the University of Suffolk. Caroline has published short stories in various anthologies including *Suffolk Folk* (2021), *Suffolk Arboretum* (2022) and *Suffolk Haunts* (2024). She holds a BA (Hons) in English and a Master's in Creative and Critical Writing from the University of Suffolk.

Angelina Klein is a published poet and author, currently living in the county of Suffolk, with a deeply intrinsic connection to its countryside. Her love of the landscape has enabled her to start writing a novel, set primarily in Aldeburgh and East Suffolk, and she hopes that her writing can one day inspire others to capture the charm and beauty of the county. Angelina is currently studying for a BA (Hons) in English with Creative Writing at the University of Suffolk. She has had various works published prior to joining the course, including an article for the *Poetry Earthlings Magazine* and short stories in *Young Writer* anthologies. She presently runs a poetry Instagram account, @apj.klein. poetry, where she takes poetry requests and shares her most recent pieces. Angelina has been shortlisted for the Student New Angle Prize 2025

Mika is a writer and student of Business and Management at the University of Suffolk. Though their academic background is in business, Mika has a deep interest in storytelling, memory, and the emotional connection people have with place. Her work often explores the quieter moments in life – those that reveal meaning through rhythm, routine, and community. In 2025, Mika was shortlisted for the

Student New Angle Prize (SNAP) for a story that captures the layered charm of East Anglia's landscapes and lives.

Ashton Turner is a current student at the University of Suffolk, studying Business Management. Alongside his interest in the dynamic world of business, Ashton has always enjoyed creative writing. He is fascinated by the power of storytelling to create compelling characters and vivid locations through just a few descriptive words. Ashton also runs his own website, Bricks Up, where he publishes daily news articles about the world of LEGO. In addition to his many brick-building articles online, 'The Rising Tide' is his second short story to be longlisted for the Student New Angle Prize.

Lauren Searle grew up in east Suffolk, where many of her favourite childhood memories were made exploring the countryside on horseback. The rural beauty and quiet character of the county left a lasting impression and continue to influence her creative work. Alongside studying for a degree in Psychology at the University of Suffolk, Lauren enjoys writing fiction, non-fiction and poetry in her spare time, often drawing on themes of place, memory, and folklore. She is passionate about encouraging others to explore and appreciate the richness of the local area. In 2025, Lauren was longlisted for the Student New Angle Prize.

Jade Darton is a writer, web developer, and Computer Science student at the University of Suffolk. Born and raised in Ipswich, their imagination has always wandered further afield. As a lifelong lover of fantasy, Jade spent their younger years with their nose in a book and their head in the clouds, most often somewhere over Middle-earth or Panem. Their writing was recently longlisted in the Student New Angle Prize 2025. Their passion for creative writing is matched by a deep commitment to LGBTQ+ representation and accessibility in online spaces. By leveraging their technical skills and creativity, Jade aims to build inclusive platforms that empower and authentically reflect their community.

Angela Nowak is a writer who has spent years juggling the joyful chaos of family life with her passion for storytelling. Somewhere between nappy changes and school runs, she managed to bring two books into the world, *Big and Brave* and *Waterman's Fire* – right alongside her five children. Poetry was something she happily left to her more talented friend and writing group leader, Julia. But when something touches her deeply, Angela is always up for a challenge – hence her decision to try her hand at writing poems herself. When she set her heart on writing a proper historical novel based on her mother's tragic childhood after the war in the USSR, she realised she'd need to support herself first and so began a long detour into nursing. While the novel has to wait, Angela shares her words on social media most days. She may not have a huge following, but she reaches one grateful reader at a time – and that, to her, is more than enough.

Creative Writing at the University of Suffolk

The MA Creative and Critical Writing at the University of Suffolk offers you the opportunity to take your writing seriously, and join a vibrant writing community, focusing on your passion for creative writing whilst engaging with debates in critical theory. On the course, you will nurture and develop your skills as a writer, reader, and researcher. Enjoy a year-round guest speaker programme, author talks and publishing opportunities while broadening your knowledge of the production and reception of literature under the supervision of award-winning writers. To find out more please go to: https://www.uos.ac.uk/courses/pg/ma-creative-and-critical-writing

OTHER MA CREATIVE AND CRITICAL WRITING STUDENT ANTHOLOGIES AVAILABLE FROM THE TALKING SHOP PRESS

SUFFOLK FOLK:
East Anglian Folk Tales for the 21st Century.

In this collection of old tales re-visioned for contemporary readers, East Anglia's green children, mermaids, malekins and monsters come together with the secret lives of fairies and the power of lost-loves, making bold new stories that leap, hagstone in hand, into modern life.

'A wonderful collection of stories of Suffolk'
–Amazon 5* review

'A perfect gift in fact, for those with an interest in original short fiction, folk lore and Suffolk.'
–Waterstones 5* review

SUFFOLK ARBORETUM:
Original Stories Inspired by Remarkable Trees.

It is possible to find every tree or area of woodland featured in these stories. We recommend you take a tour of Suffolk with the anthology in hand and find each tree, from Haverhill to Lowestoft. Sit in the dappled shade of green canopies and read the original writing that our county's woodlands inspired.

SUFFOLK REFLECTIONS:
Original Stories Inspired by the Waterways of East Anglia

The stories in Suffolk Reflections run deep through our county's precious water reserves, its rivers, lakes, ponds, streams, and seascapes. This collection of new writing is a literary love song to water. From seal-skin selkies to the silver darlings of the herring fleets, from the beam of a lighthouse to flash floods and marshland ghosts, and a woman bathing in the starry glow of phosphorescence in a midnight sea, these original stories form a shifting tide of human stories of love and hope.

SUFFOLK HAUNTS
Original Stories Inspired by the Legends
and Landscapes of East Anglia

The writing in this anthology casts a fresh eye on our East Anglian landscapes and the rich storytelling traditions that are found in the region's myths, legends, and ghost stories. From a story of ghost writer M.R. James as a boy, to the tale of a patched-up cottage with a cellar door borrowed from a storm-hit lighthouse, alongside tales of haunting movie stars, church mysteries and surprisingly lively ghosts, this anthology gathers together a rich array of tales to thrill, spook, and delight the reader.

https://www.uos.ac.uk/study/ma-creative-critical-writing/

Join us!

4583.76.453